BOYS' LIKE HER

TRANSFICTIONS

by Taste This

Anna Camilleri
Ivan E. Coyote
Zoë Eakle
Lyndell Montgomery

photography by Tala Brandeis,
Chloe Brushwood Rose & Trisha McDonald

press gang publishers
vancouver

The Publisher acknowledges financial assistance from the Book Publishing Industry Development Program of the Department of Canadian Heritage, the Cultural Services Branch, Province of British Columbia, and the Canada Council for the Arts.

Canadian Cataloguing in Publication Data

Taste This (Performance group)
   Boys like her

   ISBN 0-88974-086-0

   1. Gays fiction. 2. Short stories, Canadian (English).*
3. Canadian fiction (English)—20th century.* I. Title.
PS8235.G38T37 1998   C813'.01083520664   C98-910610-1
PR9197.33.G39T37 1998

Edited by Persimmon Blackbridge
Copy edited by Barbara Kuhne
Design by Val Speidel
Cover photograph by Lisa Poitras, © 1998
Photo-illustrations pages 73, 74, 77, 109, 111, 112, 205, 207 by Val Speidel, © 1998;
   for photography credits see page 217
Printed and bound in Canada
Printed on acid-free paper ∞

Press Gang Publishers
an imprint of
Raincoast Books
9050 Shaughnessey Street
Vancouver, BC   V6P 6E5   Canada

This book is dedicated

to my grandmother, who gave me her diaries
— iVAN

to those who dance in their own flame, and
to Mom, for all that you are
— aNNA

to freedom of thought, which transcends
all censorship
— lYNDELL

to all those who have travelled with me so far and
to those who still wait in the wings
— zOË

Contents

BENT

WET

Foreword

Kate Bornstein

Hi there, and welcome to the book. This is a collection of stories and rants and whispers and nudge-nudge-wink-winks from a group of smart, strong, truly delightful boyz and grrrls. I've seen them perform, and the stuff they talk about knocks me out. It blows me away that these writers actually got published, because they are saying, so well, stuff that most of us have been afraid to talk about. Like me, when I was a kid.

There was this one time when I was ten years old—maybe eleven or twelve, but not yet thirteen. I was sitting in a restaurant with my parents. My older brother was off at boarding school. My parents and I had just finished a big Italian meal, and I was feeling comfortably full. It took a lot in those days to make me feel comfortably full. My mother used to buy my clothes in the Husky Boy department of the discount clothing store across the tracks in Asbury Park, New Jersey. This was 1958 or '59, maybe 1960.

My father peered intently at my face. I felt the blush beginning to rise in my cheeks. Was he gonna see anything? My father, a big man, a rude man, a rough doctor of the community, my father turned to my mother, the lady, his beloved, and he said, "Mildred, your son has eyelashes like a girl."

This was one of the big forks in the road of my life. This was where I went to my deep-inside place and wished as hard as I could that my mother would say something like, "You know, Paul, you're right. He does." And then she'd turn to me and say, "Honey, have you thought that maybe you'd like to be a girl?" And me, I'd breathe a sigh of relief, I would. The kind of sigh that only a pre-teen who's been laughed at and left out for his weight and his brains and his clumsiness and his Jewishness, this little me can breathe, really breathe and I'd say, "Yes. Oh, yes … that makes the most sense to me, Mom. Thanks, Dad, for noticing." And my father would smile and say, "Think nothing of it, son—whoops! Better make that 'daughter'."

And the three of us would have laughed, just like families on television laughed together. And the pounds would have dropped off my body, and the rest of my features would have fallen into the conga line of my girly-girl eyelashes, and the next day my mother-the-lady and I would have gone shopping (not in the Husky Boy department) and my name would probably have been Alice or Allison, not Albert, and yes, that would have been that.

I wouldn't have gone through another twenty-five years of silence. I wouldn't have spent hour after hour of every waking day wondering why I was a boy instead of a girl. I would have simply reached an amicable agreement with my parents, and that would have been that.

No more hiding clothes in nooks.

I wouldn't have finally gone through with my gender change only to spend the next twelve years still looking in silence for some gender to belong to, some gender the culture approved of that would somehow include me.

No more teachers' dirty looks.

But this was not yet the freewheeling sixties. This was the if-you-don't-have-something-nice-to-say-don't-say-anything-at-all fifties. So, what really happened was my mother turned to my father there in the restaurant and she said, "Don't talk like that, Paul, please. It's difficult enough with his weight problem."

Don't talk like that.

Lots more silence, lots more fears.

Don't talk like that.

Lots more wishing, lots more tears.

I didn't talk like that. My father didn't talk like that. None of us ever talked like that. But I'm sitting here today, and I've just turned fifty years old, and I'm writing a foreword for a book that talks like that. What a joy! People are actually talking like that!

For the last eleven, maybe twelve years I've been practicing this girl thing in a fifty-year-old modified man's body, customized, designerized by surgery and hormones to resemble something roughly like a woman's body. I'm learning this whole adolescent grrl thing, I'm learning the pretty thing, but I'm learning it at the mid-century mark, and that makes me smile. When I'm not frantic, it makes me smile.

And I still look around for role models. I look around for the ones who are talking about breaking the rules, and whenever I can find someone who can tell me how they've broken the rules and the roles and they can tell me this with a grin, I wanna listen. I wanna listen to people who talk like that, who can say, "I'm a girl, but I'm a boy, I am."

I wanna listen to girls who wanna be girly-girl and strong.

That's who's in this book.

I wanna listen to the sweet boys, the gallant young gentlemen.

That's who's in this book.

I wanna listen to the truly gracious ladies.

That's who's in this book.

I wanna laugh with the slutgirls and partyboys.

That's who's in this book.

I wanna listen as more and more of today's children talk about what we couldn't talk about back when I was a child. I wanna devour their stories of abuse, misuse and gender dysphoria. I wanna hear myself, through their strong voices, tell my parents, "Yeah ... I've got eyelashes like a girl because that's what I wanna be in the world. Can we start talking about this now?"

Can you imagine a world where people felt safe enough to talk about what's really on their minds? No matter your age, your race, your class, your whatever, you could just turn to someone on a bus and start talking and they wouldn't think you were a freak. You could turn to your lover and tell hir what's really on your mind, any time. You could talk with your parents. You could talk with your children. That's the kind of world this book is pointing toward, that's what I think.

The stories in this book aren't all bouncy-bouncy happy ones. Some of the stories in here are pretty scary. Nonetheless, this book gives me a great deal of hope for the future of the world. It does. I read these stories and I think to myself, "My God ... they're talking like that, and they're writing it all down!" If it's true that writing can help shift the culture off its far-too-stable axis, what in heaven's name are the authors of this book going to be writing about in another twenty or thirty years? What kind of world will they be writing in, twenty or thirty years from now? If their stories can encourage more people to talk on this previously forbidden level of conversation, what kind of world will they have influenced?

Once you've read these stories, will you talk more about what you were once forbidden to speak? I hope so. I hope you get some good courage from reading this stuff.

I want to close by saying I hope you enjoy this book as much as I have. Because as scary and forbidden as these stories might be, each of the writers has managed to find a voice that speaks with great dignity, great gentleness, grace and gallantry. If the authors of this book were my sons and daughters, I would be bursting with pride over each and every one of them. They've given the culture a lovely gift in this collection of stories.

OK—read on. And the next time someone close to you opens a scary topic of conversation, I hope the courage you'll have gotten from this book will help you handle yourself with great dignity, great gentleness, grace and gallantry. That's what I got from reading these smart new writers. That's what I wish for you. Go on—enjoy!

Introduction

Taste This

We didn't set out to write a book.

We got together quite by accident in November 1995 to do one show, a spoken-word, storytelling, boot-stomping, fiddle-playing experiment in a small theatre in East Vancouver. We were four individual performers: Lyndell, a musician; Anna, a wordsmith; Ivan, a storyteller; and Zoë, an actor. But when the lights came up we rubbed off on each other like paint in a car crash. Something happened when our words bounced off each other and the audience. Together we made each other ... well, better. Somehow it all worked and people laughed, and they clapped, and they listened. That was all the encouragement we four stage-sluts needed. We borrowed a car, borrowed some time, made ten pounds of pasta salad and took the show on the road.

Somewhere in the midst of all this chaotic bliss Persimmon Blackbridge slipped us her phone number and encouraged us to try to imagine a page as our stage.

A live performance exists only in the moment. You get up there with your best shirt on and your boots polished and you do your thing. The audience laughs or not, cries or claps, and then the house lights come up and everybody goes home. A book is a different story. You are alone with yourself and your computer, and you write and rewrite, because once your words are printed, bound and published, they're not just yours anymore.

There are things you can't get away with in a book that you can on the stage. A winning smile won't help you. Nor will the right sort of pause ... at exactly the right time. Spell-check takes on a whole new importance. When putting the book together we tried to hold onto the live-show-on-the-road roots of our connection to each other. Woven into the stories we tell on-stage are the stories that got us there, the experiences we shared, the questions we asked and the immediacy of a story told under a spotlight with our comrades mouthing our words behind the curtains.

Including photographs was a way to capture the performance energy. The photography has been a give-and-take, back-and-forth collaborative process with three photographers who are also our friends, our colleagues, our partners in crime. Some of the images were shot with fast film under bright stage lights; others were pro-duced specifically for this book. Each was chosen with a specific emo-tion, story or energy in mind. In some cases the images inspired us to write more. What an exciting process—to struggle with words and then see a photograph that provides the period, the breath, the con-tinuation of a much larger conversation. Chloe Brushwood Rose, Tala Brandeis and Tricia McDonald each brought her talent and vision to these pages. It's true: a picture is worth a thousand words.

The world where our stories exist does not have hard and fast boundaries. It is a place defined by our own queries, where genre, gen-der and generations are malleable, and where transgression is often the way to transformation—transfictions.

These stories are about home, about leaving it and finding it somewhere else. These stories are about identity, about peeling off labels and slipping across borders to get at our own truths, to write them down and lay ourselves open on the page. These stories are true, except the ones we made up. They are written by four women, except when we're not.

But a show is only a show when the lights dim and the audience listens. After cuts and edits and spell-checks, after meetings and soul-searching and a thousand and one midnight phone calls, these stories are missing one thing only. They are waiting for you to turn the page.

bound

Border Crossing: No Proof

Ivan E. Coyote

All four of us were crammed into one car—I don't remember who we borrowed it from that time—about to cross the border back into Canada. We were all riding on a great-show-lots-of-praise-good-food-even-better-friends-going-home-now kind of feeling, and I personally was not prepared for what was about to occur.

Call me a nationalist, but I *expect* to get hassled entering the States, I have always equated America with the authorities that be, but I considered getting back into Canada to be a somewhat kinder, gentler cavity search. So I found myself shocked when they hauled us over.

We had followed all the rules: Lyndell and I were looking about as respectable as we ever will, both wearing clean white button-up shirts and black Levi's. Anna was proudly Canadian in her kilt and long socks, and Zoë was wearing that nice-guy, face-splitting smile of hers. I personally wouldn't suspect her of being up to anything suspicious, even in striped and numbered overalls and with half a pair of handcuffs dangling from one wrist.

We had rent receipts, phone bills, proof of employment and paperwork for the cigarettes we had bought and declared. So why were we all so nervous?

We were clean. Just four upstanding citizens going back home to resume contributing to the gross national product. Thank God I didn't know at the time that Anna wasn't wearing any underwear under her kilt.

hy were we all so nervous

I am not famous for my cool-headedness in times of crisis, but I learned the hard way that the best thing to say to men with guns and blue shirts is "Yes sir, of course, sir," politely and with as much feeling as possible, so that is exactly what I did.

Because this is the law. They have every right to paw through my journal with latex gloves on, scattering love notes and photos and preciousness and privacy all over the trunk of the car. They have every right to take Lyndell's irreplaceable violin out of its case and place it, helpless, on wet concrete, while they slide their sausage fingers through its velvet-lined home.

So we stand there and smoke, and take turns consoling each other as each of our bags is systematically turned out by Mr. Leer and Mr. Peer.

I remind myself to breathe, remind myself that they will never find what we are smuggling across the border.

We are, after all, the very criminals they assume us to be.

We are carrying contraband words with us, memorized, tucked away in tattered journals and stored magically on disks in Anna's left pocket. Canadian words, queer words that we spoke on-stage for money in the land of the brave. With no valid permit, licence, visa or contract to do so.

Felons, really, all of us, and now we intended to flee the scene without paying income tax on the twelve dollars and fifty American cents we each made. It's just this kind of shameless law-breaking that gives all poets a bad name.

Fortunately, you cannot smell poetry in the car afterward, it doesn't leave any residue in the lining of your pockets, believe me. Poets are hard to pick out of a crowd, and storytellers are even more elusive and hard to catch in the act. There is no urine test for musical ability, so they were forced to let us go. Even though they knew we were up to something.

Four queers crossing the border in a borrowed car, four smiling and self-satisfied queers, were most certainly up to something.

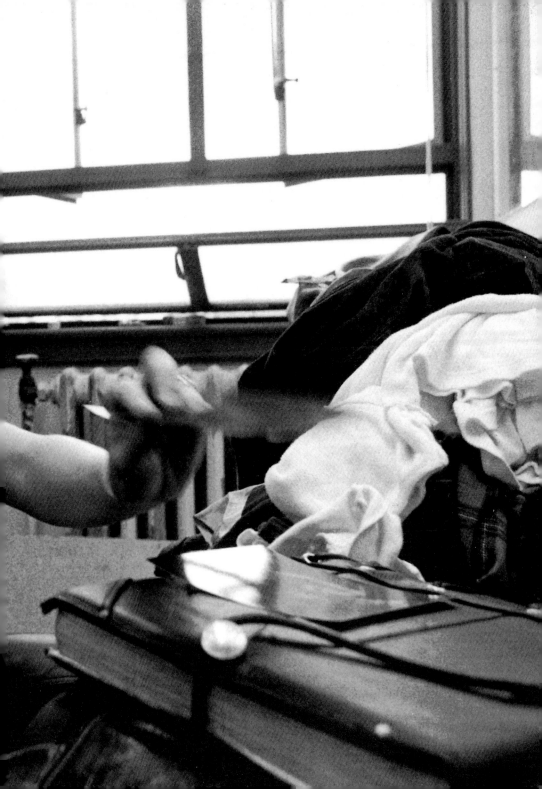

No Bikini

Ivan

I had a sex change once, when I was six years old.

The Lions pool where I grew up smelled like every other swimming pool everywhere, that's the thing about pools. Same smell. Doesn't matter where you are.

It was summer swimming lessons, there was a little red badge with white trim that we were all after, Beginners, ages five to seven. My mom had bought me a bikini.

It was one of those little girl bikinis, a two-piece, I guess you would call it. The top part fit like a tight cut-off T-shirt, red with blue squares on it; the bottoms were longer than panties but shorter than shorts, blue with red squares. I had tried it on the night before when my mom got home from work, and I found that if I raised both my arms completely above my head too quickly, the top would slide up over my flat chest and people could see my you-know-whats.

"You'll have to watch out for that," my mother had stated, concern making lines on her forehead. "Maybe I should have got the one-piece, but all they had left were yellow and pink. You don't like yellow either, do you?"

Pink was out of the question, we had already established this.

So the blue-and-red two-piece it was going to have to be. I was an accomplished tomboy by this time, so I was used to hating my clothes.

It was so easy, the first time I did it, that it didn't even feel like a crime. I just didn't wear the top part. There were lots of little boys still getting changed with their mothers, and nobody noticed me slipping out of my brown cords and striped T-shirt and padding, bare chested, out to the side of the pool.

Our swimming instructor was broad shouldered and walked with her toes pointing out. She was a human bullhorn, bellowing all instructions to us and punctuating each sentence with sharp blasts on a silver whistle that hung about her bulging neck on a leather bootlace.

"All right, Beginners, everyone line up at the shallow end, boys here, girls here, come on come on come on, boys on the left, girls on the right."

It was that simple, and it only got easier after that first day. I wore my trunks under my pants and changed in the boys' room after that first day. The short form of the birth name my parents bestowed on me was androgynous enough to allow my charade to proceed through the entire six weeks of swimming lessons, six weeks of boyhood, six weeks of bliss.

It was easier not to be afraid of things, like diving boards and cannonballs and backstrokes, when nobody expected you to be afraid. It was easier to jump into the deep end when you didn't have to worry about your top sliding up over your ears. I didn't have to be ashamed of my naked nipples, because I had not covered them up in the first place. The water running over my shoulders and back felt simple and natural and good.

Six weeks lasts a long time when you are six years old. In the beginning I thought the summer would never really end, that grade two was still an age away. I guess I thought that swimming lessons would continue far enough into the future that I didn't need to worry about report card day.

Or maybe I didn't think at all.

" 'He is not afraid of water over his head'?"my mom read aloud in the car on the way home, her voice rising at the end of the sentence. My dad was driving, eyes straight ahead on the road. " 'He can

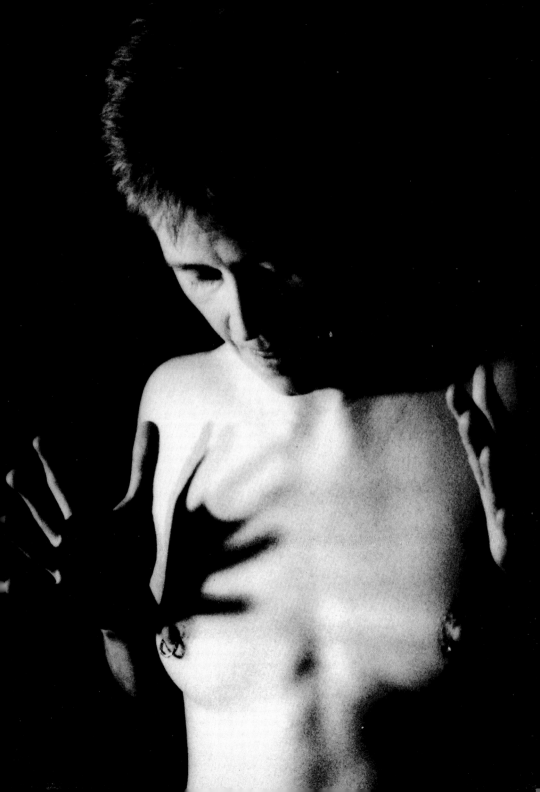

tread water without a flotation device'?" Her eyes were narrow, and hard, and kept trying to catch mine in the rearview mirror. "Your son has successfully completed his Beginner's and Intermediate badges and is ready for his Level One'?"

I stared at the toes of my sneakers and said nothing.

"Now excuse me, young lady, but would you like to explain to me just exactly what you have done here? How many people have you lied to? Have you been parading about all summer half-naked?"

How could I explain to her that it wasn't what I had done, but what I didn't do? That I hadn't lied, because no one had asked. And that I had never, not once, felt naked.

"I can't believe you. You can't be trusted with a two-piece."

I said nothing all the way home. There was nothing to say. She was right. I couldn't be trusted with a two-piece. Not then, and not now.

Pigs & Twats

zoë eakle

I can't remember a time when I didn't think about sex. I imagine the question "How did I get here and how will it affect the rest of my life?" occurred to me about the time I came streaking out of a perfectly warm womb into my father's awkward hands on a rainy West Coast night.

By the time I was three we had moved to the semi-deserted tip of the small island where I was born. The woods I grew up in were deep and magical. Sex there was more a fact than curiosity. Everything lived and died in its own good time, and death always gave way to new life.

On one side of those woods was a lighthouse with red-and-white government buildings and perfectly manicured lawns as short and trimmed as a dyke's fingernails. But if you wandered through those woods, they spilled you out into a whole other world. A world where the grass was long like hippie hair, bleached out, standing on end and blowing in the breeze, as thick and rich as a healthy hemp plant. It was Eden, post carnal knowledge and anti-industrial revolution. There a hard-working young couple lived in a do-it-yourself A-frame built from wooden beams, cedar shakes and rubber tires all held together with early twenties newlywed hope.

There they fertilized their sunny California back-to-the-land consciousness and raised me, a sturdy little creature barely taller than the grass itself. At that time I referred to my vagina as my twat, with-

25

out shame or hesitation, and I never wore pants in the summertime because it didn't feel good. I remember first consciously contemplating the sexual act when I was five. At that point fucking meant life, and babies, which also meant death. Somehow they were all tossed together like the ingredients in the use-it-all stews my mother served up for dinner. I knew I was wrapped up in it somehow, served up on the plate of life along with everything else. Now you have to understand that my life was never at stake, but I was raised on a farm and for almost every living creature in captivity that's just how the cycle went.

Take, for example, the pigs. Guy mounted girl and gyrated about wildly like a drunk in dirty spats trying to walk a straight line, doing an absurd dance that made my friends and me laugh. It looked like

slapstick physical comedy at a Vaudeville sideshow. A coupla months later out came those slippery pink blobs thick with mud and birth slime and oh, aren't they cute, but ya know, we raised 'em to eat 'em so momma pig suckled them for a coupla weeks and the next thing ya know, *bam!* it was slaughtering time. With the quick fall of an axe blade that separates this life from the next, momma and papa pig were hanging headless in the back yard. I mean, what would *you* think? This was no *Charlotte's Web.* The spiders undoubtedly wove strange messages in their webs, I believe they always have, but they never said in plain English, "Save the pigs."

I understood at an early age the wonder of nature, but I also knew its potential harshness. There were things that just happened, seemingly for no reason—unfair, unasked for, harsh consequences

brought about by the hand of nature and humans alike, as inevitable and unforgiving as a winter's storm. It seemed strange to me that nobody ever talked about these things.

There were three things delicately steered away from in my presence. Three things only alluded to, never broached in any detail. They were fucking, birthing and dying. Now I knew all three happened and I figured they must all be connected because they all produced jokes with punch lines I didn't understand. Whenever I asked for further explanation—usually from my father, who usually told the jokes—it produced an embarrassed little dance involving the awkward shifting of weight from one foot to the other, and very little in the way of actual information. I soon learned, however, that I could score as much as a quarter from my father on these occasions if I brought up the inappropriate topic and then promised to cease and desist if a little coin changed hands.

My parents were more liberal than most, though, being back-to-the-land flower children, so whenever they finally decided I had asked enough embarrassing questions, they did their best to answer them. That is, they bought me a book. Now in the book the man climbed on the woman and as far as I could tell they did it pretty much the same as the pigs did, with pretty much the same result. Except when they did it they had wide open spaces to frolic in. First they walked hand in hand under a full moon (this seemed important) and they had warm dry grass to lie in and a glorious sunset in the background. It was very picturesque: altogether cleaner and more civilized than anything I had been witness to. Well, I knew that was bullshit, for a start, because I'd heard my daddy's grunts and my momma's moans (it was not a large A-frame), and there was nothing clean or civilized about their noises. They were as silly, incomprehensible and embarrassing as the pig dance, and just as fascinating.

Now in the book the woman had long flowing hair and the man had a perfectly coiffed Clark Kent cut, and even when they were done there wasn't a hair out of place. Seeing as how my mom had short hair which was generally neat, while my dad's hair was long, I natu-

28

rally wondered what logical conclusions could be drawn from this. I wondered, for example, if it had any effect on who mounted whom. So, I went to my dad for clarification.

He was chopping wood in the front yard when I found him. His T-shirt and his long hippie hair were both wet with sweat. The whole fertile vastness of the garden lay before us and the pigs were grunting in the background, pawing at the dirt with their cleft hooves and nose-diving for treasures in the mud. I followed the swift fall of the axe splitting fragrant timber into chunks small enough to fit in the wood stove that cooked our supper and said, "Dad?"

"Yeah Zo."

"Since Mom has short hair and yours is long, does that mean she goes on top of you?"

The axe stopped in mid swing, then came slowly to rest on the chopping block. For a moment he did what I had come to recognize as the traditional foot-shifting dance around the three unmentionables, and then he looked at me as though he'd lost something, some small object like a hammer or a tape measure he was sure he had placed there only a moment ago. "Could you repeat the question?" he said.

I did, and well rehearsed, I might add. He gave me a long, level look. "Have you done your chores?"

"Yeah."

He nodded and gazed intently at something above and behind me. Then he began to study the chopped wood as though he might find the answer there, as though if he stared at it long enough it might grow lips and answer me for him. Finally he stroked his beard and said in the age-old manner of fathers imparting sexual wisdom to their daughters, "Ah … your mother's milking the goats out back, why don't you go ask her?"

I examined his face for anything further and, receiving no clues, I turned to go. As I disappeared into the rhubarb patch between the front and back yards Dad called out to me, "Hey Zo!"

"Yeah?"

"Tell me what she comes up with, will ya?" he grinned.

"Sure," I said, and smiled the same smile back, the one he gave me at conception. I was pleased because I figured there might be as much as a quarter in there somewhere if I held out a little and played my cards right.

I strode into the back yard with a sense of confidence. Mom was good. She could handle almost anything with a minimum of foot shifting. Her information was usually fairly accurate, if somewhat baffling. Mostly, I had just wanted to see what Dad would say first. If I could score one quarter before we took the speedboat to town next, I'd have to choose between a comic book and a chocolate bar. If I managed to score two, I could get both.

My mom was milking Daisy when I found her. Daisy was my favourite goat. She was one of the animals I was allowed to get close to because she wasn't up for slaughter. She was there for her milk. In return she would be allowed to retire in peace one day, a friend of the family. I watched my mother's strong fingers coax thin jets of Daisy's creamy milk into a tin pail.

My mom registered my presence without looking up. "Hello there," she said, and continued milking.

"Mom?"

"Mmm?"

I repeated my question to her exactly as I had to my father moments before. She didn't look up but the milk flowed more thickly as she laughed. "You asked your father first, didn't you?"

"Yeah."

"And did you pilfer all his spare change?"

"No ... not yet, he wants to see what you say first."

"Oh I see, he does, does he? Well, I'm sure you'll tell him whatever you like, but hair length has nothing to do with it."

"Does he climb you then, like the pigs do?"

She laughed. "Well, I guess the first thing you should know is that there's pleasure in it for both of us or I wouldn't have anything to do with it. It's not exactly what the pigs do, either, although I suppose I'd have to admit there are certain similarities."

I tried to equate the pig dance with something pleasurable like pancakes on Sunday, swimming in the ocean or going to town in the speedboat to buy comic books and chocolate bars, but I couldn't make a connection, and I needed one. A deep concern furrowed my five-year-old brow. "Mom, what if he climbs on you and you don't want him to?"

Her hands were steady, her voice level, goat milk flowed. "Well, first of all, he doesn't, and second of all, I'd make it very clear. I'd start with 'No' and I'd end with 'Fuck off.'"

My mother never minced words much. If I had been picturing my father, perhaps I wouldn't have had such a hard time fathoming what my mother said, but I had pigs on the brain and I couldn't imagine that determined little dancer in dirty spats stopping his Vaudeville shuffle for anything. "What if he still doesn't listen? Then I guess you'd cut off his head and hang him in the back yard like the pigs, huh?"

My mother finished milking Daisy, took her time wiping the excess milk from the overworked teats, and finally turned to me. For the first time her voice had the slightest hint of an edge to it, like the knives she would sharpen on a flat, wet, grey stone. "Anyone ever refuses to take no for an answer, you show him the door and do whatever it takes to make sure the bastard never crosses your threshold again." I nodded soberly. I knew two things at this point: one, it was important to her that I appear to understand what she was saying, even if I didn't; and two, this particular conversation was officially over.

We were silent for a moment, she contemplating me and I contemplating her words. Then I turned to go. "Hey Zo," she said.

"Yeah?"

"You're five years old, for Christ's sake. Enjoy being a kid."

"Sure," I said and skipped off through the hippie-hair grass to see if I could squeeze a quarter out of my father.

I wasn't aware of it at the time, but my mother's eyes must have been full of me then. Full of everything it takes to be a mother and everything that nothing can prepare you for when you serve a child up into this world.

I'm not sure I understand any more about sex now than I did as a five-year-old running around with my twat open to the four winds and watching pigs fuck in a pen under summer skies. I haven't stopped asking embarrassing questions, though. I know now as perhaps I didn't then that sex is a way of discovering all the roles I can play and how those roles can change. It is a real and insatiable urge, like pigs doing a dance so vital it makes me laugh. Surrounded by concrete as we are, it seems we are still nature's beasts, bound by our animalness to an animal act, intimately connected to death, reborn every time we come, rushing into the unknown, birth slime and all.

Children know these things, even if they don't understand them. They know them because the whole living, breathing world vibrates with carnal knowledge. And I'd bet my daddy's last quarter they know they're wrapped up in it somehow. Served up on the plate of life, along with everything else.

Sparrow

Anna Camilleri

Unlike other adults, who warned about the dangers of lighting matches leading directly to blazing fire, my grade five teacher, Ms. Cormack, did not speak a word about danger or safety. While standing in the centre of the room, our desks in a semicircle, she struck a match and touched it to the wick. Flame. The smell of burning sulphur tickled my nose, a smell I would grow to love. She held a saucer over the votive. The flame flickered, became smaller. Her breasts rose and fell with her breath. She raised the saucer higher with great ceremony. The flame grew. Dropped the saucer on top of the votive and the flame promptly went out.

"Do you know why the flame went out?" she asked.

The room was silent. She, the powerful sorcerer; we, the adoring pupils. My mind raced with possibility. *The flame went out because she willed it to. The flame went out because it was done burning. The flame went out because it was the only flame in the room.*

"Fire needs oxygen to live, breathe and grow. Without oxygen there is no fire. We need it to live. We also need fire. You'll learn more about that later. All in good time." Her eyes sparked mischief.

She didn't speak to us in the manner that the other adults did. No condescension or frilled words ending in question marks. Her voice was hot caramel, ice, polished silver. There were rumours about her; each day brought a new one, more involved than the previous. Everything from former careers as an opera singer, stripper, spy, to

33

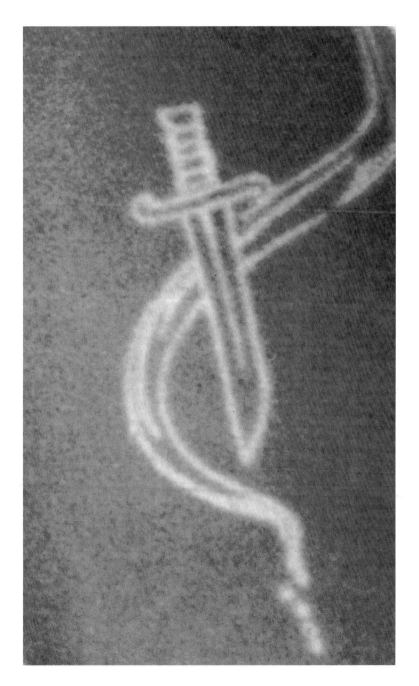

36

travels around the world where she had lovers in waiting. I'm sure (not entirely) that most of the rumours were just that—brilliant fabrications. There were no rumours about any of the other teachers. They didn't inspire them. Ms. Cormack incited stories, dreams, fantasies, desire—even lies. She was the kind of woman who caused lovesickness, complete with fever, delusions and madness. I imagined being one of her lovers, eagerly waiting for her next word, touch, glance. I had no idea what the word lover meant, but I wanted to know. I wanted to feel that deeply. Most of all, I wanted to become a woman like Ms. Cormack. Graceful, beautiful, intelligent and coveted.

Ms. Cormack was struck by on-coming traffic on Richmond Street, eight years ago. She spent two days in Toronto General Hospital's intensive care unit with massive head injuries. Her last words were "Let me go." Seeing her in a casket, waxen and still, would have been sacrilege. She did, however, love ritual—loved to create it—and her funeral, complete with incense, candles, choir cherubs, a eulogy and formal attire, was the ultimate performance. But she was not the mistress of ceremony, and for that reason, I could not attend.

Even at the time of her death, there were those who believed that she didn't die—that it was either a grand mistake or a staged performance. A whole new crop of stories was harvested. Some say that she is now a gargoyle living atop a gothic building at the site of the accident. Others believe that she is eating grape leaves in Greece. What do I believe? I remember the day she caught me drawing a portrait of her in my lined notebook during science class.

"Is that a picture of me, Anna?" she smirked. "Well, you've given me remarkably large eyes. Eyes are interesting. The camera was designed on the original model, the human eye. Let me show you." She sketched an eye. "Here is the retina, the iris, the lens and blood vessels. The pupil expands and contracts to let more or less light in … You can change your view of the world by squinting your eyes or turning around." I squinted at her. Her face fluttered and twinkled like the sun straining to shine through cloud cover. She laughed at me. "Oh Anna, there is so much to learn." She looked like she was

37

thinking of faraway places. "All I ask is that you listen before deciding you're not interested."

"Yes, I'll listen ... Do you think eyes are windows to the soul,
Ms. Cormack?" I never called her by her first name. She never
granted us that privilege.

"Well, I suppose that's possible. It depends on your view."

To this day I remember the names of clouds because of her:
cumulus, cirrus and stratus, with variations like cumulonimbus, alto-
stratus, etc. My inclination toward the romantic could have led me to
a dreary, self-indulgent belief that she lives in the heavens where the
clouds are, but I know better. She's the stuff that lava is made of, not
rain.

Once she referred to Mary Magdalene as the whore who Jesus
loved. A shiver ran up my spine. I imagined Mary Magdalene holding His cock while He kissed her feet. The principal walked into our
classroom just as she spoke those words, *the whore who Jesus loved*. The
next day, a substitute teacher wearing a bun, starched collar and knee-
length skirt instructed us to move our desks into rows and told us to
call her ma'am.

I learned two things the day the flame went out. One, if I am ever
trapped in a burning building, I will not open a window. I will stare
out through the glass, luxuriate in the heat, and like a patient spar-
row, I will look toward the sky. I will think of Ms. Cormack and hope
she hears me. Two, desire is powerful, mysterious, beyond science.

Three Left Turns

Ivan

The air shimmered and twisted where it met the earth. The road beneath the tires of my bike was a ribbon of dust, hard-packed and hot, a back-road racetrack, and I was gaining on him.

His BMX was kicking up a cloud of pretend motorcycle smoke. I smiled and pedalled through it, teeth grinding grit and lungs burning, because the stakes were so high. If I won, I was faster, until next time, than my Uncle Jimmy. And if he lost, he was slower, until next time, than a girl.

Is the little brother of the woman who married your father's brother related to you? I called him Uncle Jimmy, regardless, and he was my hero.

He was four years older and almost a foot taller than me, and I don't think I ever did beat him in a bicycle race, but the threat was always there.

Just allowing a girl into the race in the first place raises the possibility that one might be beaten by a girl, so the whole situation was risky to begin with. We all knew this, and I probably wouldn't have been allowed to tag along as much as I did had I been older, or taller, or a slightly faster peddler.

Girls complicate everything, you see, even a girl like me, who wasn't like most. You can't just pee anywhere in front of them, for instance, or let them see your bum under any circumstances, or your tears.

even

a

girl

like

me

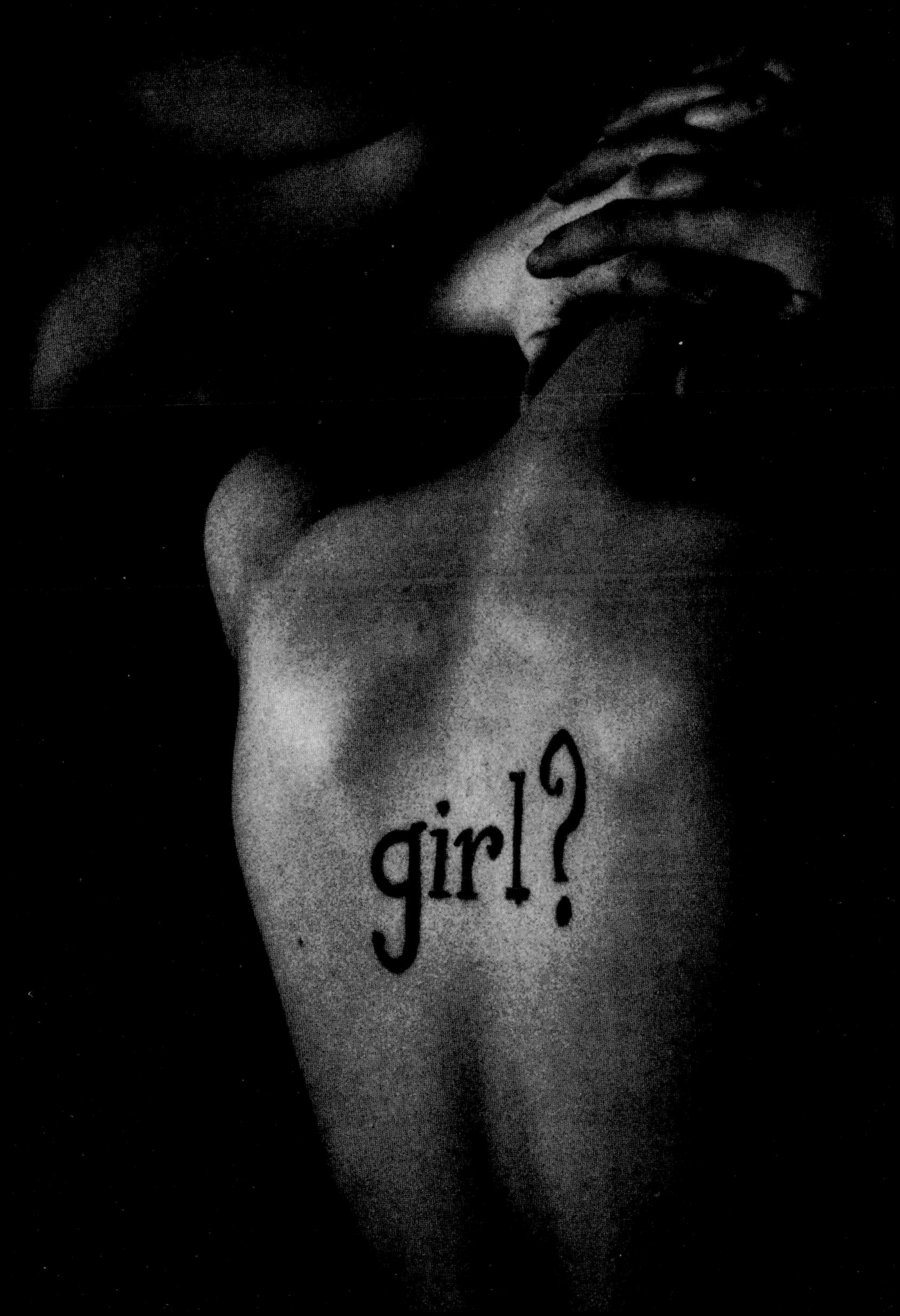
girl?

There were other considerations too, precautions to be taken, rules to be observed when girls were around, some that I wasn't even privy to, because I was, after all, a girl myself. It was the summer I turned six years old, and I was only beginning to see what trouble girls really were.

But I, it was allowed by most, *was* different, and could be trusted by Jimmy and his friends with certain classified knowledge. I was a good goalie and had my own jackknife, and could, on rare occasions, come in quite handy. Like that day. That day I had a reason to tag along. I had been given a job to do, a job vital to the mission.

The mission was to kiss the twins. For Jimmy and his skinny friend Grant to kiss the twins.

The twins were eleven, and blond, and from outside. Being from outside was a catch-all term used by people from the Yukon to describe people who were not from the Yukon, as in: *Well, you know how she's from outside and all, and always thought she was better than the rest of us,* or, *I couldn't get the part and had to send it outside to get it fixed, cost me a mint,* or, *well, he went outside that one winter and came back with his ear pierced, and I've wondered about him ever since.*

The twins were blond, and from outside, and were only there for the summer. Their dad was there to oversee the reopening of the copper mine. They wore matching everything, and also had a little sister, who was seven.

That's where I came in.

The plan was a simple man's plan, in essence. As we worked out the details, we all stood straddling our bikes in a circle at the end of Black Street where the power line cut up the side of the clay cliffs.

We were all going to pedal over to where the twins and their little sister lived. We had already hidden the supplies in the alley behind their house. The supplies consisted of a small piece of plywood and a short piece of four-by-four fence post (Jimmy and I had two uncles who were carpenters, and he would himself go on to become a plumber).

We would take the plywood, prop one end of it up with the

not girl.

four-by-four, and build a jump for our bikes. Then we would ride and jump off it right in front of the twins' house, which was conveniently located right across from the park (good cover). This would enchant the unsuspecting kissees-to-be (and most likely their little sister), drawing them out of their house and into the street, where they would be easier to kiss.

We would then gallantly offer the girls a ride on the handlebars of our bikes, having just proven our proficiency with bike trick skills by landing any number of cool jumps. The girls would get on our bikes, and Jimmy and Grant would ride left down the alley with the twins, and I would take a right with their little sister, keeping her occupied while they carried out the rest of the mission. The kiss-the-twins mission.

The only person more likely to tell on you than a girl, after all, was her little sister. But I had it covered. Keep her occupied. Don't tell her the plan. Don't wipe out your bike and rip the knees out of her tights. Drive her around the block a couple of times, and drop her off. Grant and Jimmy would take care of the rest.

We thought we had pretty much everything covered. We even had secondary strategies. If the jump didn't work right away, we could always make it higher, and if that didn't work, I could bravely lie on the ground right in front of it, and they could jump over me.

It was a good plan, and it worked.

What we hadn't foreseen was unforeseeable to us at the time. The girl factor, that is.

How could we have known that the twins' little sister would think that I was a boy? And how had the girls already found out that Jimmy and Grant wanted to kiss them?

And what was I supposed to do if this girl, who was one year older than I was, slid off my handlebars as soon as we rounded the corner into the alley, planted both of her buckle-up shoes in the dust, and both her hands on her hips, and wanted me to kiss her like my uncle was kissing her older sister?

It hadn't crossed our minds, but that is exactly what she did (and I can't remember her name to this day, and can't make one up, because this is a true story). The twins' little sister wanted me to kiss her, and I'm sure I must have wanted to oblige her, if only for the sake of the mission. Because that is the first most secret, sacred tomboy rule: never chicken out of the mission.

There was only one problem. The girl problem. She didn't know I was one.

It wasn't that I had deliberately misled her, it just hadn't really come up yet. And since me kissing anyone was never part of the plan as I knew it, I had not given much thought to the girl factor. But this girl had a plan of her own.

There she was, all puckered up and expectant-like, and it seemed to me I had a full-blown situation on my six-year-old hands. A mistake had been made, somewhere, by someone, but what was it?

I had a number of options at that point, I guess. I could have put my left hand on the back of her yellow dress, my right hand over her smaller left one, and given her a long, slow …

No, I would have dropped my bike.

I could have leaned awkwardly over my handlebars and given her a sloppy, short one, and just hoped for the best, hoped that there wasn't something about kissing a girl the boys couldn't tell me, any slip that might reveal my true identity. I might even have gotten away with it, who knows? And I would have liked for this story to have ended that way.

But it didn't. And because this is a true story, I would like to tell you what really went down with me and the twins' little sister in an alley by the clay cliffs the summer I turned six.

But I don't remember.

What I do recall is that unexplainable complications had arisen due to us not taking the girl factor into consideration, and that rendered this mission impossible for me to carry out at the time.

According to Grant and Jimmy, when the dust had cleared and the little sister found herself alone in an alley in this weird little town where her dad made her come for the summer, she started to cry and the twins had to take her home.

45

And two weeks later when all three left, unkissed, Grant and Jimmy still considered me a major security risk. But I don't remember my retreat.

My Aunt Norah, who was seventeen at the time, was babysitting us that day. She said I came flying up the driveway, dumped my bike on her lawn, streaked past her into the living room, and threw myself on the couch, sobbing incoherently.

I would like to think that at this point she patted my head, or hugged me, or did something to calm me down, but we weren't really that kind of a family. It's not like I was bleeding or anything. She said that when I finally calmed down enough for her to ask me what was wrong, all I could say was three words, over and over.

I don't know. I don't know. I don't know.

Girls. We can be so complicated.

ZOË

Lines, we all have lines, words, we have crafted words. words we want people to praise us for. words we want delivered just so, with a certain inflection, a tone, the right sort of pause. Having them memorized makes it even better, gives more freedom, more room for dramatic impact and inflection. I am the least daunted among us when it comes to remembering pages of text verbatim. That's because I learned to be a word sponge during four years of acting school. I keep trying to tell my cohorts that they're a lot like actors: hopeless hams, addicted to the spotlight, fond of their own voices and perfectly capable of memorizing their own work. we challenge each other and then pay for it dearly.

Ivan is currently memorizing "Lord Love a Dove," in which I play the part of his subconscious, the implications of which might alarm me if we weren't already living in each other's armpits. He has embarked upon this exercise fearlessly and with great vigour. He has asked me to pick up the cues of his subconscious—in moving vehicles, at roadside cafés, outside the washrooms at rest stops. All this is fine. This is what we do for each other.

We're heading to Seattle tonight to set up for a show. Ivan's just about got that story cased. It'll be ready to go for sure. we get to the performance space, otherwise identifiable as an artsy-fartsy café with friendly staff who are willing to set up chairs in such a way as to create a stage. we settle last-minute details and make our way to the homes of our respective billeters. Now, intimacies among the individual members of Taste This being what they are, Lyndell and Anna often end up across town or across the hall from

ivan and i, who inevitably end up in various degrees
of close proximity blanketed in the warmth of broth-
erhood and the nervousness and excitement of an upcom-
ing show. seattle was like this, he and i in a double
bed, at midnight, lying side by side discussing
entrances and exits and lighting cues, after he has
recited his piece one last time. but it's late and
we've got a big day ahead of us tomorrow.

    "goodnight, brother."

    "goodnight, man. it's gonna be a great show." he
curls up to his pillow on his side of the bed, i curl
up to mine on the other. rest stops along the way form
a backdrop in my brain, the forefront going over
lines, blocking, those few last props we have to somehow come up with before the show.

    finally, slowly, sleep begins to creep in between
the words and claim my consciousness. as i'm drifting,
my brain begins to softly recite "lord love a dove,"
except it's ivan's voice. my eyes open wide on my side
of the bed.

    "ivan?"

    "yeah?"

    "shut up or i'm going to kill you."

    "sorry man, sorry. just want to get this thing per-
fect, you know."

    "i know."

    "ok, sorry man, goodnight."

    "goodnight." ah sweet silence....

    "do you want to do the lines of the subconscious
just once?"

    "ivan!"

    "ok, ok. goodnight. jeez."

Blood & Salt Water

zoë

Standing on the back porch on the 25th of December, just after midnight. I guess it's the 26th now. I guess it's over for another year, all the hoopla and marketing, nuclear family stress and ceremony. I'm looking down on the silk-white snow under a perfectly clear starlit sky. I'm smoking a cigarette under the eyes of the moon and wondering where you are. Maybe it's all the Christmas carols I've been hearing lately. They're everywhere I go, in restaurants, banks, on street corners, I can't seem to escape them. Remember that Christmas Eve two years ago when we hitchhiked out of the city across the water to that small patch of old-growth rock and grass where we used to play truth-or-dare in Uncle Pat's old Chevy truck? It's permanently parked now by that shed out back where you offered me my first real smoke, boards greyish green with weather and determined moss.

That day when we went home you stood up front with your brightest shade of fierce red lipstick on, thumbing the rides. I waited in the background in my heavy boots with my cap on backward, the other half of a roughly packaged deal. The roles we play are laughable, we know them so well. It was my natural duty to stress the time factor. We couldn't afford to wait between rides for more than an hour total.

You said, "Trust me, we'll be home by the 6:10 ferry." You even insisted that we stop for lunch at some deep-fried roadside café along the highway. When we finished eating you took your time freshening up in the pine- and puke-scented bathroom and came out with a

verything from a fast fuck and cl

fresh coat of lipstick on and your naturally white blond hair artfully dishevelled. You pulled a smoke out of your black leather bike jacket and lit it. We made the 6:10 with an hour to spare.

We ended up at your mom and Uncle Pat's place that night, face to face with the full spread: aunts, uncles, cousins, even your little brother was there. We were the prodigal daughters come home to the hopeful smiles of our mothers and their kin. Your mom's best tablecloth was spread out over two tables in the dining room, laden with turkey, potatoes, candied yams, Brussels sprouts, cranberries and gravy, and of course there were Christmas carols. "Through the years we all will be together ..."

You were still living on the island when I first left home for the intellectual flatlands of my university career in Toronto. I shook my head and laughed when I heard you'd shacked up in a little house that Douggie built for you. You'd always had the best-looking deckhands and treefallers in town on your doorstep, offering you everything from a fast fuck and clean coke to a lifetime of commitment complete with two kids and a steady income. It figures you'd pick the wildest bad boy on the island, referred to by my parents as every mother's nightmare. Two years later he had been converted by your mischievous smile into a full-on planning-for-the-future kinda guy that even your mother was beginning to like. I imagine it was right about then that you said something to the effect of, "Baby, I been noticing that this island is real small and surrounded by an awful lotta water. A person could drown in all that water." And you were gone within the week.

One Christmas, I think it was my third year in Toronto, my mom bought me a plane ticket home. The night I arrived my mother and I sipped wine in her and Gerald's tiny kitchen while Gerald was out helping Uncle Pat drywall his new place. My mom was cutting up sundried tomatoes for spaghetti sauce. I was in charge of making the salad and was asking questions about who had done what while I was gone. I asked how you were. She said you'd sent a letter from San Francisco. She smiled, "Sounds like she's doing really well. Now she

49

coke   to   a   lifetime   of   commitment

asked me not to mention this to Gerald but she said I could tell you."
My mom spoke with juicy mother/daughter confidentiality, artfully
casual and knowing. "You'll never guess …"

"She's gay." The words slipped out of my mouth without into-
nation or cause. If you'd asked me at the time how that word applied
to my own life I would have said, "Live and let live." If anyone had
asked me if you were gay I probably would have shaken my head and
laughed just like I did when you moved in with Douggie. I would've
been imagining all the robust young men who would mourn you, saying, "But she was such a pretty girl." As though you'd died. It surprised me as much as my mother when the revelation that she'd been
leading up to with such delicacy and suspense came out of my mouth
as though it were the most obvious thing in the world.

My cheeks flushed and I concentrated on shaking my carefully
mixed vinaigrette, acutely aware that my back was to my mother and
that I was in no hurry to change that. I could feel her eyes analyzing
my shoulders and willing me to turn and face her. "Yeah, how did
you know?"

"I don't know, I just know. I mean, I don't know, really. I could
be wrong. Am I wrong?"

"Nope."

I tossed green leaves of lettuce into the air, watching them land
and coat themselves in vinegar and oil.

Three years later I'd done my time in Toronto and I guess you'd
had it with the girlfriend and whatever else you had going in San
Francisco. I stumbled across you at the wharf in False Creek dressed
in familiar scaly gum boots, Stanfield shirt and overalls, your shoul-
der-length hair slipped through the back of your baseball cap in a
ponytail that grazed your neck when you walked and exposed the little shaved part underneath. The fishing season was over and you
needed a place to stay so we shared an apartment in East Van for a
while. When I talked to Gerald on the phone one night he asked if
we were lovers. When I stopped laughing I asked him what the hell
inspired him to ask such a question.

He said, "Well, since you're both, you know, and people talk a lot around here, it's just a rumour I heard."

"Come on, Gerald, you've known us both since we were in diapers, what do you think?"

"Well, I figured that it probably wasn't true, just thought I'd ask. So how's work?"

As I was hanging up the phone I tried to imagine you and me as lovers. No offense, couz, but I still couldn't stop laughing long enough to get my head around it. As far as blood goes I guess there'd be nothing terribly kinky about it.

It goes like this. Your mom and my dad went to university together in California. Your parents convinced my parents to come and raise their newly emerging family in this little bit of barely touched perfection. Our mothers' love of the island outlasted both their marriages and they stayed on to plant trees and pack fish while our fathers became university professors who had once, when they were young, lived off the land.

Eventually our mothers found new partners, a coupla hot-headed Irishmen, both with an irreverent sense of humour and strong, reliable work ethics, slightly red necks and hot tempers. They had all this in common most likely because they happened to be brothers and that's the island for ya. That's your Uncle Gerald and my Uncle Pat. So there's no shared blood between us but when you've seen as much of each other over the years as we have, when you've played nasty practical jokes on each other and defended each other when no else would, blood is a mere formality.

I couldn't afford to go home for Christmas this year. It was my first year ever on my own. I made time-and-a-half wages, though, washing dishes at a burger joint, sweeping chunks of leftover turkey and stuffing out of an industrial sink with latex-gloved hands. I walked home under late-night streetlights shining on freshly fallen snow. My only moment of real sadness was when I called home and no one had heard from you.

So where are you tonight? Where have you been for the past year?

There are rumours, distant and disheartening, disconnected, contradictory and ill-informed. Drugs have been mentioned, so what else is new? We've raided more than a few poorly guarded greenhouses together in our time and since then we have both swung high on the monkey bars in a chemical playground. Sooner or later, though, you hit the swings and after that it's the seesaw and that gets boring real fast, up, down, well, you get my metaphor. Drugs and guns together, that's new, new connected to your name, connected through history to my own. I don't care about the drugs or even the guns. I assume nothing. I question everyone who thinks they know anything. Whispers tell me that everything has changed, that I would not recognize the woman you've become. But I have seen you become many things.

The last time anyone saw you your lipstick was on crooked and the whole of you was small enough to fit in the palm of my hand, brittle enough to be broken if I hugged you too hard. I imagine you crushed, none of you left to hold on to.

52

When it comes right down to it, I wonder what I always have: What are you running from? Why have you never told me and how come I know anyway?

So, what now? Will the next rumour I hear make me shake my head and laugh? They'll say, "You'll never guess how she got herself outta this one." If I could find you, would it make any difference? Or is it just for me, this searching, so I can look in the mirror and soothe my self-important reflection for doing its level best to bend your undauntable will to my own, to keep our paths separate but parallel somehow. If I could ask you all these questions would you say in a tired, earnest voice, "Just back off"?

I blow smoke into still silent air and let my eyes wander out over that deceptive crystal covering that makes everything look so soft, blanketing all the sharp edges and pitfalls to a rolling plane that bounces off the moon and makes the world bright in the heart of darkness. I sing the one line of that cheesy Christmas carol that I remember still. "Through the years ..." Ah, whatever. I've always hated Christmas carols, especially at Christmas, they get stuck in my brain like a broken record. I spend the rest of the year rinsing them out of my head just in time to be bombarded with the same four chords and cheesy sentiment.

I tell myself you're fine, and begin waiting for next year. I'm always amazed at how quickly those Christmas carols come around again. Maybe next year will be the year we both make it home again. We'll take a bottle of island moonshine out onto the north shore to a beach party with a blazing bonfire like the kind we lived for in high school, and I'll ask you where the hell you've been. You'll tell me some crazy story and I'll tell you you're full of shit and you'll laugh and turn to me with the warmth of the liquor racing down your throat. You'll flash me a coy red lipsticked grin and say, "Hey there, little boy, don't forget who gave you your first cigarette."

LYNDELL

If there is any such thing as a person who is an expert at saying goodbye, I don't want to meet them. I don't need to learn how to be stoic. I want to know exactly what it feels like to love someone enough that tears just come. I want to be unsure about what the future holds.

We are not the type to stay in the same place, get good government jobs and raise families. We are thrill seekers, with strange connections to pavement that stretches out to the next, to the next, to the next . . . town. We all love to ride the road of possibility. This is a good thing. But to say "Goodbye, my lovelies" . . . hurts.

Remember San Francisco? The last stop on our west coast tour, it seems so long ago now. Our tight budget that afforded us the luxury of many cheap bean burritos and water to swish them down. Remember the shows that people actually came to even though no one knew who we were? Remember sleeping in small places and laughing a lot? Remember not talking about the fact that Zoe was leaving us indefinitely? Remember the morning when we sat on the front stoop of Inka's house drinking coffee, smoking cigarettes and watching the people walk by on their way to church? I've

never seen such astounding outfits in my life they were
as colourful as all the skies we'd passed under during the
past month that was the morning we left you there, zoe,
standing by the bottom gate and waving as we pulled away
from the curb pointed north, heading home you were to be
without home for the next seven months and we were to
be without you i missed you already i missed your sopra-
no voice rounding out the sound of our road songs on that
long drive home that was only the first of many goodbyes
to come

youreturned from abroad only to find that anna and
i didn't live in vancouver anymore and that ivan was
hitting the road to possibility, and there you were,
back home and we were gone

i suppose saying goodbye means that we will say
hello again and the embrace will be as beautiful as
those colourful outfits that walked by the four of us
sitting on the stoop it will be as rich as the skies
that we have all walked under this last year and a
half it will be as though we'd never been apart,
except that we will all have new stories to tell as
we sit around a table, drink cheap wine, make toasts
and laugh until the sun comes up and there is yet
another sky

Mother Faith

Lyndell Montgomery

I call her every Sunday from my den where I sit and drag lightly on cigarettes. She talks to me from the phone bench right outside her kitchen. I know she can see the flourishing garden and fruit trees scattered throughout the yard. I imagine her in a Sunday dress with her hair slightly askew, legs crossed, ankle twisting in a circular motion, the cat rubbing up against her. This Sunday I see her so clearly, sitting there three thousand miles away swinging her foot 'round and 'round, hypnotizing her. Talking while picking the garden from beneath her nails.

She tells me everything and nothing at the same time and I wonder how it is possible that I understand. She does not offer explanations, she offers words that I dig through, rip out of sentences and paste together. She tells her story in camouflage. She tells her story through silence. In between her description of how the morning-glory is taking over, the sparrows squabbling outside the kitchen window, the quote she got for new carpet in the living room and who was missing in church this morning, silence is heavy. In these moments, I listen. This is when she tells me she loves me, she misses me, she is sorry. Silence on the phone is laden, fertile, and like the land that lies between us, full of history.

I suck tar and nicotine into my lungs and feel it burn itself into my cells. I wonder why I still smoke. I wonder, as I look out the den window into the neighbours' back yard littered with rusting cars and

too much garbage, why I don't live near mountains and ocean. I think of how different my view is from hers. How different it has always been even when we looked out the same window.

I know so much about her, this woman who raised me to be everything I am not today, and in that knowledge I am weak and infant. I am not married, pregnant or silent. I do not pray for forgiveness, though sometimes I wonder if I should. I do not fit the mould she cast for me. I never did, but I needed her.

An eye for an eye. I was never her little girl. Never the one to help her bake or plead for dresses and new dolls. I was never there for her to act out her version of motherhood. I was gone.

My brother, her son, is also gone. He was stone like her. He never had anything to tell her and she never asked. Afraid of answers, questions by-passed, the same as childhood. My mother was left childless. Left with a husband's rage, and Faith. Steady, strong, sure, absolute Faith.

The elongated pause on the phone makes the distance between us more apparent as the connection crackles in our ears. "I like it when you call in the afternoons," she says. "Dad is always taking a nap so we can talk without being interrupted. I don't really like having him on the phone, I can't get a word in edgewise."

I think of him and instantly feel overwhelmed. There is so much to hate, to be angry about, but what is hate and anger other than cancer slowly and precisely eroding me? I'm not sure if it is her whom I forgive, or if it is God. And how can I forgive God? God is supposed to forgive me. But I do forgive Him for my mother's entrapment. She believed so vehemently in the Way, the Truth and the Life that reality staring her right in the face in the form of a hurt seven-year-old child was not seen. Truth, black-and-blue bruised truth on my face, arms and legs, produced nothing more than long prayers from my mother to God as she knelt by her bed each night.

I sip lukewarm tea and listen. "The magnolias are as refreshing as ever and the corn patch, goodness, it's growing like crazy. Of course the raspberries are also ripe so I went out after meeting

she tells her story in camouflage

and picked a few handfuls to go with waffles for lunch. We would have enjoyed a fresh garden lettuce too but the slugs are taking over ..."

She continues talking. I close my eyes and see the garden, alive underneath the summer sun. My ten-year-old eyes scan the rows of peas hoping she'll see me and call out as I walk carefully through the back yard. In her bent position, she doesn't notice me. She is busily picking weeds that are choking vegetables. I enter the house as quietly as possible but ten minutes later I am on my back picking which ceiling tile to escape to. How could she not know?

"... The garden relaxes me. It's quiet there. The earth feels good, cool between my fingers. You know how sweaty my hands always are." I imagine my house with stacks of Top Twenty records and cassettes, laughter and wine with dinner and friends over during the day. Maybe even sleepovers. Making up rock-and-roll songs on the piano, playing dress-up with borrowed lipstick, shearing my hair to a brush cut. My fantasies are smashed like the china we ate off when company came for dinner. I flash to the memory of Father in a rage, hurling dishes across the dining room. My mother can see the marks left on the wall from where she is sitting right now.

I imagine him lying in bed, the mattress sagging beneath his weight. I wonder how he can possibly relax enough for sleep to overtake him. Does he have nightmares? Images of someone sneaking into his room armed with a baseball bat?

I remember Sunday mornings. My small hands bending folding chairs back into their storage position. Women in long dresses walk out the door with uncomfortably clothed children in tow. Men are hanging back in the hallway, talking. Someone is thinking of buying a new truck, others are bantering over specific models and whether or not to get air conditioning. I don't want them to leave, but slowly they trickle out the door offering last words with their backs turned and halfway down the front stairs. Father shuts the door and bolts it in place. I carry the chairs to the hall closet, small arms aching from the weight of the load. Father is outside now burying the remains of

61

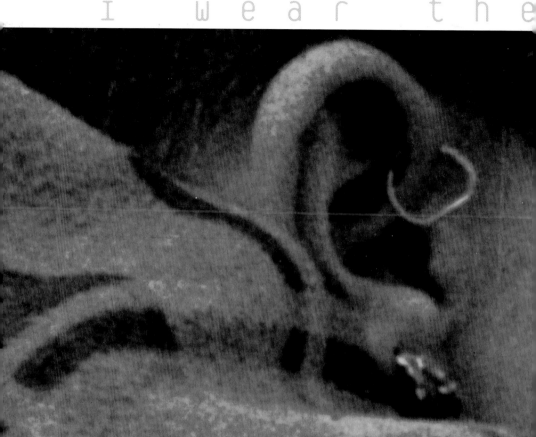

62 the bread which resembles the body of Christ in the garden, for mother to resurrect.

The doors of the shed screech as they resist closing and Father's footsteps sound on the back stairs, the door opens and shuts in one movement and just like that the happy family façade is laid to rest for another week.

Mom, wearing a conservative dress from D'Allaird's, is flitting around the kitchen, preparing lunch. Her hair is pulled back tightly in a bun, loose strands hanging over her tired face, tickling her.

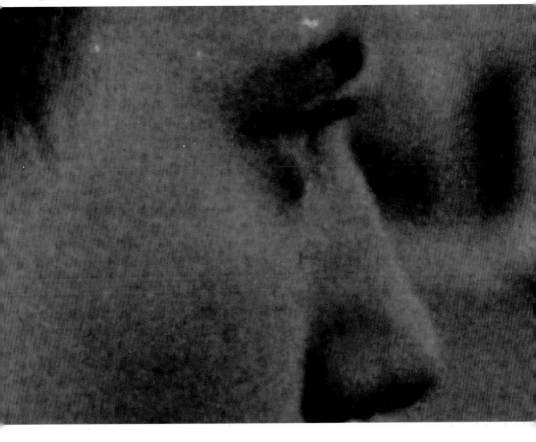

Father starts subtly today by mentioning how beautiful Melva's hair looked braided carefully with bits of heather.

I set the table in silence, jaws clenched. Mom hurries from the kitchen with a steaming bowl of garden beans in hand. We sing grace and pile our plates with food. We eat in silence except for the smacking sound of father's lips. I am cringing. I feel like he is chewing on me, grinding me into a fine powder. I am being swallowed. Washed down with a swig of cranberry juice.

I gag on the silence and before I know what is happening, words fly from my mouth, hitting my father square on the jaw. He counters with a slap to my head and a fist. I wear the bruises like I wear clothes. Every day.

I wonder what they talk about now, just the two of them sitting opposite each other at the dining room table. Do they even talk? Mom never used to.

I can't say for sure what made her just sit at the dining room table silently picking at her food while my brother was out breaking into someone's house and I was two inches off the ground, suspended like a puppet with my father's hands around my throat. Maybe she had learned that if she opened her mouth in protest, she'd be next in line for restructuring. Maybe she'd had her share and now it was my turn to take it. She cried when she got hit, I never did. I can't imagine her burden. Her cross so heavy and humiliation just around the corner if she moved to help me.

She stayed because it was the only way she could go to heaven. I left because I wanted to stay alive. I was thirteen the day I slipped out the front door.

"Not too much else exciting to tell you about," my mother says. She has moved me through the garden, her week at work, church and the dog's health. I hold the phone tightly to my ear. "I'll call in a week," I say and we hang up with soft goodbyes. I know that next Sunday we will talk about much of the same. Still, I call, hoping that this will be the week she will begin to tend life, like she tends her garden. I grind out my cigarette and think of her life, her faith. I am confused and crying.

My mother will never leave my father. My father will always hide his violence behind God. My brother will never apologize. My family will never again sit in a room all together and I will never be the child in the house that I fantasized. But time passes and bitterness melts like winter. I never could stand the cold.

Incarnadine
Anna

Wind blows cool through the side door, ajar just a crack. Breaks up the curls of smoke drifting through light cast by the fernels overhead. From my place on the stage this is all I can see, dancing smoke curls. The audience, a faceless echo. I hear their laughter, whispers and programs fanning beaded faces with smeared mascara. Freshly brewed coffee, sweat from skin dressed in leather, amber and sandalwood, these scents waft.

Words roll out of my mouth; the undertow pulls me away. *Today my grandfather was sentenced to prison.* No, don't think about that. Think about the road trip back to Vancouver. Hope that crossing the border won't be a pain in the ass, but I know it will be. It always is. Think about the list with sub-lists and starred items that waits on my desk. I'm moving to Toronto in ten days. Three thousand miles away. The garage sale is tomorrow. So much to do. I'm selling all of my things, some precious, some disposable. Shipping is too expensive. How many times have I done this?

I've wandered too far from shore. The audience is a ship in the distance. I swim upstream like incarnadine salmon, break through the surface to the stage, the heat, my final words: "All I see is red." I follow the applause off-stage where the air is cooler. Where there is room to breathe. Where I can swim without measuring distance.

I'm an expert at packing, having moved more times than I can count on both hands. There is always a good reason to move.

Negligent landlord. Crazy neighbours. Expensive utilities. Relationship break-up. The need for a new view. There's a rhythm to the ritual of sorting, packing, unpacking, like the moon's cycle. I'm accustomed to it. I appreciate the weight of a full box. With each move, I discover forgotten letters and embarrassing photographs. Everything old is new again and everything new is old enough to be packed. Bare walls, a fresh start in need of a TSP treatment and paint.

My friends have crossed out and replaced my number in their phone books at least eight times. *Cheers to your new place and to friends who are stupid enough to help you move again ... Hey Anna, how about a toast to fresh latex!* I chip in *Yeah, yeah, I've sorted my stuff more often than you've cooked this year.* Bright voices bounce off the bare walls. We eat greasy pizza on milk crates. Drink warm beer. I imagine how my apartment will look, estimate dimensions, count phone jacks and guess at where the studs are. Scribble notes inside my cigarette pack for the trip to the hardware store. Everyone goes home to their beds, cats, dogs, lovers. I throw a sheet on the futon, crawl under, light a candle, sleep.

I have moved exactly seventeen times, in two different provinces, in the past nine years. There have been many lovers, new neighbours, garage sales. Nobody asks me what I am running away from. I would be indignant. On a crowded bus when a stranger's elbow is up under my chin, I ask myself. *What are you running from?* I always come to the same answer. I'm running *to*, not from, *to*. I hold fast to this answer like an exhausted swimmer gripping a raft. I swim some more. My stroke improves. I rest at the next island, dazzled by the view. It cycles like looped videotape, like the moon, like the seasons. The waters between the islands begin to feel familiar, then the same, routine, confining.

I've lost things between moves. The watch my grandmother gave me for my Confirmation. Many pairs of socks. A few beloved plants that really didn't like moving. An iron, which I never used. A rake and garden snips. My name has remained. And my dreams.

I used to insist, "I don't dream." I lied.

*   *   *

This morning I jumped out of bed before my lover was awake and began telling her about my dream, nudging her till her eyes were open and blinking.

I am sitting in a concrete yard, leaning against a fence, naked. You walk through the gate and hand me twelve smooth, whittled branches and a sea sponge. You are dressed in army fatigues. In a very businesslike manner, you tell me to put the sponge inside my cunt and then to embed the branches. I am calm and attentive. You explain that in case of rape, the bastard will get pricked, pull out and run away bleeding. I spread my legs, insert the sponge and branches, and whistle into the traffic. No one notices my lack of clothing, not even you.

She sat upright and touched my face gently, distressed. "It's a good dream," I explained. "I'm not scared. I didn't wake up shaking." When I was a child, I had nightmares about hooded men clawing at my bedroom door, trying to break in. I always woke just before the door was kicked through, in a puddle of warm piss. Sometimes I dreamt about rats, hundreds of rats, gnawing at the walls and ceiling. My body was stiff. I lay in bed, looking up at the swirly plaster motif. I couldn't stand up. I imagined my dreams to be hovering around the light fixture, like flies. They waited until nightfall, until my lips parted, until I looked like a babe in a crib and then, only then, the hooded men and rats descended.

*   *   *

I stopped pissing my bed when I was sixteen years old. I'd had enough of soggy sheets. My doctor, a fresh-faced twenty-five-year-old just out of college, told me I had a common condition, enuresis, which is caused either by emotional trauma or a physiological problem. He asked if anything traumatic happened to me when I started bed-wetting. I said no, then yes, recalling my first surgery, then the words spilled out, "My grandfather molested me." My body folded at the waist. The room spun. I held onto my tears, straightened and looked at him. He leaned forward, his face screwed up in a confounded, empathetic expression. I didn't want his kindness. I wanted to get away from those words, from myself. Gathered my bag and darted. I walked aimlessly through the city, convinced that everyone in the world had heard me. The streets were unusually loud, littered. When I arrived at home, my mother asked where I'd been. I said nowhere. And under my breath, nowhere and everywhere.

I stopped dreaming about hooded men and rats after I filed sexual assault charges against my grandfather. I consider my dreams to be "normal" now. I dream about whistling kettles and large warehouses filled with kinetic sculpture. I dream about swimming in the Mediterranean Sea, in Maltese waters.

I first thought about filing charges when I was twenty years old. But I was not ready for a messy family crisis. Not ready to speak the details aloud. Two years ago, I visited Toronto and walked through the neighbourhood I grew up in. "Running to, not from," had begun to feel like lead weight hanging from my shoulders, a show of strength for everyone but me. I walked past my grandparents' house, the house where it all happened, where they still live. Apart from some minor exterior renovation, their house is preserved, as in my memory. I wanted to open the door, run into my *nonna's* strong arms, to savour the sweet scent of her skin and the errant hair from her French bun that used to tickle my nose. She would set out provolone and asiago cheese, pannine, prosciutto, antipasto, espresso, red wine. I would protest, saying I had just eaten and she would push the plate toward me and exclaim, *"Mangia, mangia!"* But now I couldn't bring myself to cross the street. I had told my grandmother what her husband had done to me. She had turned her cheek, let my words fall to the ground, like leaves. Those leaves, slippery, brown and rotting, I could not cross.

I ran into the wind, rounded the block and sat on the hill in my elementary school yard. That hill seemed so damn big when I was a child. I remember standing at the top of it, holding a flattened cardboard box in the dead of winter. Took a running start, jumped on my magic carpet, flew all the way down and spun out at the bottom where the snowdrift started. Wax-coated vegetable boxes worked best. From the top of the hill, I could see everything.

My classmates are running, laughing, some are rolling marbles by the schoolhouse. I am leaning against the fence at the yard's edge, kicking at stones, watching, waiting for the recess bell to ring so I can go inside, out of the cold.

       ☼   ☼   ☼

On October 2nd, 1995, I filed a victim impact statement with the Vancouver Sexual Assault Squad. My words were recorded in a small room. A dictaphone and a plastic flower arrangement sat in the centre of the table. The room felt cold. A cop asked me questions. "I don't want to put words in your mouth but I need to be able to pass information on to Metro Toronto ... We need to know exactly what type of assault. What happened? ... This occurred more than once? ... Do your parents know? ... Do you have any brothers or sisters? ... Do you need a break? ... If your grandfather were here today, what would you like to tell him? ... Why did you wait until now to file charges? ... Are you employed?" The transcript is fifteen pages long. My answers were unfocussed, long-winded. "What was the question?" I asked repeatedly. What was the question? When he offered a break, I declined. I couldn't stop. I would have left.

    I wanted to scream at him, "What do you mean by that lame-ass question? Isn't it obvious why I didn't jump up ten years ago to come and tell you, a stranger, about everything that's made me nauseated for my whole fucking life? You want answers? Yes, my parents know. I told them when I moved out of their place. I have one younger brother. Not that it's relevant, but yes, I'm employed. Have been since I was fifteen. I was raped by my grandfather. No, I haven't forgotten a thing. I have a full-colour picture album. Want me to describe it? He did every disgusting thing you can imagine, and stank of tobacco, cheap wine and brilliantine. Threw my underwear clear across the room. Once? For seven years, at two assaults a week, I was raped over seven hundred times. Still had my baby teeth in. Now that

I've told you all my secrets, would you like to trade places? Tell me about the hundred ways your heart has been broken. Tell me."

I didn't yell at him. He is not the man who hurt me. In a strange way, I wished he had been. Had I been able to voice all of my pain, anger, betrayal, fear directly to my grandfather, and be heard, I would not have needed to tell my story to a stranger. But I would not have been heard, and I am afraid, to this day, of being in a room alone with my grandfather.

I signed release forms to have documents retrieved, spoke with the investigating officer three times a week. That was just the beginning. I began to feel afraid while having sex, and then stopped having sex for several months.

Those months stretched out like a cracked Prairie highway, September indistinguishable from April. Context is everything. I have been stubbornly proud of my sexuality, when it would have been more highly regarded if I had fabricated modesty. To anyone who has looked down on me from a moral high ground, I say "I am not not a lady. Never have been, don't care to be." I have flirted unabashedly. I've been hungry, demanding and patient, have taught more than a few lovers how to please me in no uncertain terms.

When my grandfather assaulted me, I was a stone: cold, rigid, inflexible, pulseless. When he finally let me go, I would run into the bathroom, lock the door, wash my hands and face and pleasure myself. I discovered the vibrating scalp massager, the pulse of the detachable shower head, the power of my own hands. I taught myself how to come in three minutes flat, while squatting, lying or standing. I fantasized about heavy petting with Deanna Troy from Star Trek, oral sex with the northern Italian girl who lived next door, restraining and straddling Mario, my classmate who bullied anyone younger or smaller than he. I learned how to luxuriate in my body, coming slow and easy. When my wrist got sore, I developed motor skills in my left hand, alternating easily. This was my revenge on the whole damn world. Short of locking me up and throwing away the key, no one, not my grandfather, not the nuns at school, not the neighbour-

70

hood signoras, no one could stop me from coming or thinking about it. Every time I came, I proved that I was alive. He hadn't taken everything. A lot, but not everything.

*   *   *

    I waited for the first long-distance phone call after I filed charges. It was my mother. I held my breath, fearing that once and for all I would be motherless. She choked out words, "I love you Anna. I'm so proud of you." My mother had never before told me that she was proud of me. I scrambled for a roll of toilet paper to mop my streaked face. She asked if I was OK. I said yes. I lied. That's all I could say. We had played our parts so well, so fully; she the wretched, unloving mother; I, the spiteful, rebellious daughter. We had been far apart and moving in tandem all along; afraid of touching each other for fear of seeing our own reflections, of the shame that threatens to pour down like a dark, open sky every time we look into each other's eyes. I step closer. "I feel shaky, but I'll be OK. Are you OK, Mom?" She assures me, "I've managed for this long," drops her voice to a whisper. "I'm sorry, Anna. I wish I could have done something. I was a terrible mother. I'm sorry, I'm so sorry." Through a tight throat I whisper, "Mom, Mama? Listen to me. It's not your fault. I love you, Mom. Always have."

*   *   *

    On the day my grandfather was sentenced to three years in a federal penitentiary, I was performing with Taste This in Seattle. Had I

71

been able to click my heels and make a wish, I would have chosen to be anywhere but on a stage with everyone in the audience waiting to be made to laugh, to be turned on or pissed off. I had nothing to give. But I couldn't bail. I took the stage. Paused for a couple of seconds, feet solidly planted a foot apart, tall posture, head high, looked around the room, and started. No introductions, no banter. I was not a performer that night, I was a conjurer, in two different places simultaneously, on-stage speaking words, "I don't want to hear one more erotic lesbian poem about pulsating petals, pink and lavender, shimmering in the sun," and in the courtroom hearing my grandfather plead guilty.

I came back to my body during the last line: "All I see is red." The audience was laughing, applauding. I said thank you and walked off-stage. I was floating somewhere above the crowd, somewhere above Seattle. I have found a place for my ability to disconnect and recreate a moment. It's true, the show must go on, and I love this.

The guilty verdict ran through me, winded me, like a blistering snowstorm. The bones of my life exhumed for everyone to see. But a part of me has always been here, out here, in the middle of a storm, in the middle of the ocean. A part of me is cold, untouched. And the truth is, the part of me that is untouchable should never have been touched. This is obvious. What is plain to see is often forgotten. So I will say it again. The part of me that is untouchable today should never have been touched. The verdict, guilty, does not change this. What it does is align the world with the truth I have known all my life. I believe that truth is what sets stars on fire, for all of us to gaze at, to wish upon, to remember.

I swim in stormy waters. The waves take me in, push me up again. I am aware of electricity, how it crackles over the ocean, a pot ready to boil. It doesn't matter. I swim. When the waters are calm, I float on my back and blink into the sun. Tumble and dive like a seal. I come up for air and breast stroke toward the next island.

ANNA

"what do you do on stage? is it poetry or what, anna?" my brother's face is wide with questions.

"joey, i don't have time to explain. we write. we perform ..." i feel flustered. what if he hates my work? what if he hates all of the people i love? was i out of my mind saying yes, of course i'd love you to visit! everything my brother knows about me—queer, dyke, artist-type stuff—has been theoretical. we've never spent time together outside of my parents' home and now he's in vancouver, visiting my lover and me in our bachelor apartment, right in the middle of a tour which sets us up in shady bars and artist-run spaces where lots of freaks show up, 'cause we're freaks too.

"ok, fine. i don't want to stress you out. i just want to be prepared if you're going to put a nail through your nose. "

"joey, what are you...?"

"or take your clothes off or something like that. 'taste this' isn't a very conservative name. you must do something interesting on-stage."

"i don't know how to describe what we do. it's per-formance.... we have lots of meetings."

"well, that tells me a whole lot of nothing." he's smiling, enjoying my skirting.

"joey, i'm nervous about showing you my life and i didn't realize that until i picked you up at the air-port."

"oh please, you don't have to take care of me."

"all right then. you're going to meet lots of peo-ple you haven't met before."

"yeah, that's obvious. look anna, you've been my sister my whole life, right?"

"right."

"so, maybe i know more about you than you think i
do. you've always been wordy, but everything doesn't
have to be said. know what i mean?"
"not really."
"all i'm saying is i know you're not a garden variety queer."
"now you're really stressing me out. where the hell
did you get the term 'garden variety queer'?"
"you're not the first queer i've met .... i do work
in interior design."
"oh well, then you must know a lot about queer culture, for a straight boy."
"shit. you're waiting for me to screw up. do you
have to be so defensive?"
"i'll try not to be."
"just because i'm straight doesn't mean i'm garden
variety either. 'dyke' doesn't necessarily mean women
who have sex exclusively with women, right?"
"for some it does, but not in my world .... besides,
distinguishing between who is a man and who is a—"
He interrupts me.
"you were talking to a looker in the coffee shop,
but you didn't introduce me."
"what?"
"she was checking me out."
"oh, i get it. just for the record, the apartment
is small and i don't want to be in it while you're
shagging a friend of mine."
"well, i guess we have a problem on our hands. you
know what they say .... like brother, like sister."

74

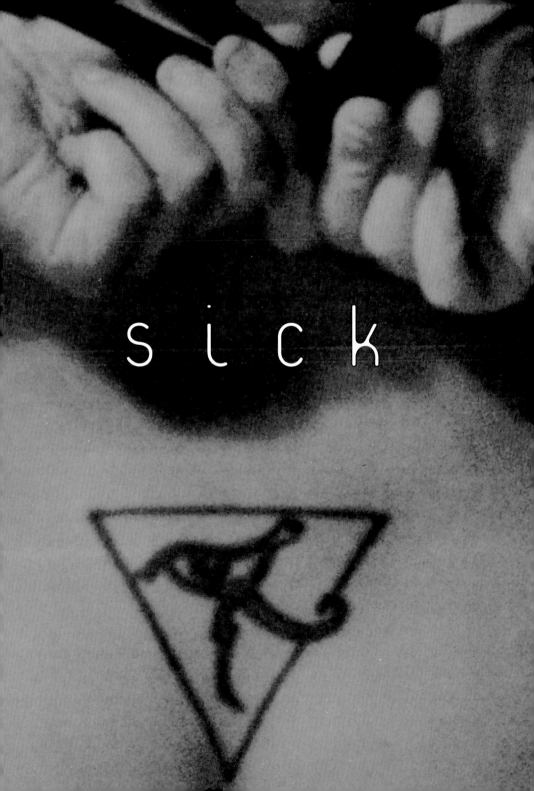

sick

Border Crossing:
Lyndell
On the Edge

We are all sitting on cold cement blocks at the Canada/U.S. border crossing. We are being detained and our car is being searched. It's not a terribly cold day (Anna is wearing a kilt), though when you're nervous, the elements always seem more acute. We sit, we stand, sit again, pace a bit, talk anxiously amongst and to ourselves. Ivan is smoking a cigarette, another sign of nervousness. The two ex-marines ripping our car apart notice our nervousness, so they slow their pace even more and begin to take articles of clothing, books, make-up cases, etc., out of the car.

I stroll over, trying to appear nonchalant in my approach. "Excuse me, guys. There's a violin in the back of the trunk that is worth a lot to me. If you decide to take it out, please let me do it for you. I'd be happy to open the case, anything you want, just please let me handle the violin." They respond with grunts, both their heads buried in the contents of our trunk.

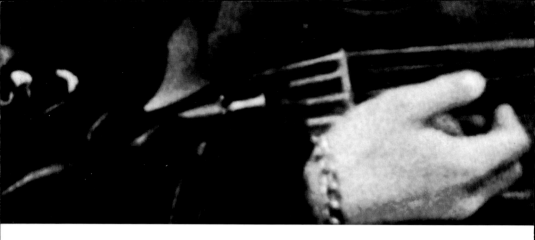

I return to my place on the cold pillar. The gang demands to know what I said, so I tell them and we fall silent, watching strange hands touch personal objects, hold up sex toys, flip through journals and writing material, stopping to read.

I'm pissed and justifiably so. Zoë echoes my anger with her own spoken thoughts. "Are border guards specifically trained to be as fucking rude as these guys? Are they so threatened by people like us that the only way they can gain any sense of worth is by trying to make us feel like shit? Or are they pre-programmed in the womb to end up ripping lives apart and degrading others?"

Our voices are rising, the talk is about power imbalances and a sense of importance tied to something as fucking stupid as being able to wear a jacket that says Police. Our discussion is heated and easily heard by the goons holding the power right now. The words "assholes" and "swollen cock" litter the air around us. Anna tells us to shut up and launches into a speech about us giving them what they want by acting like we are. Like kids who've been grounded we slink to the cement block and sit down. Mouths shut. Anna informs us of the time she was crossing the border only to be detained and strip searched, thick gloved fingers shoved in and up orifices. I'm raging. So what if we look like freaks, so fucking what. I hate the fucking border, it's an obvious reminder that human nature and the desire to feel superior has kept us from evolving as a whole species. Right now I find it hard to believe that the nineties are liberating.

"The fuckers, what do they think they're doing?" I shout. Anna and Ivan grab my arms, Zoë stands in front of me. My violin lies sprawled on the ground as cars which have successfully avoided interrogation drive by. "Let go of me, that's my fucking violin lying there and they're ripping my fucking case apart. I told them I'd be happy to do anything they wanted with it and the fucks ..."

Anna stares into my reddened face. "Lyndell, calm the fuck down right now. Stop thinking about yourself. I'm not wearing any underwear. I have a kilt on with no underwear. Can you understand why I'm not feeling very lippy right now? Sit down and shut up so we can get the hell out of here."

My arms are still being held and Ivan begins telling me that they've been reading his writing and he's not flipping. Zoë mentions that they've rooted through everything in her bag, writing included. I open my mouth again to defend my anger. Anna says, "No underwear, Lyndell, remember that."

The goons look in our direction. "You can go," one of them says.

"Thank you very fucking much," I reply with the hatred of an erupting volcano. We repack clothes and journals and my violin. I put her back into her velvet case, the velvet pulled and stretched, detached from the case itself, and all for what, I wonder. So every time I open it I will be reminded of exactly how small I am and how big the ocean I swim in is.

"Fuck," I say, snapping the case shut. "Another example of white collar crime has just been witnessed here."

"Testify," Ivan belts back.

Zoë salutes to the north. "Canada," she says and sighs. Anna tells me how lucky I am that she didn't get strip searched. I make a mental note to buy her underwear and lots of it for Xmas. We pile into the car and drive onward.

This is the truth, the entire truth. Not a version of. It has not been altered or adapted in any way.

Piano Keys
Lyndell

As I knelt on the stairs, praying for strength to make it to my locker, I did not entertain the thought of death. I was trying to claw my way, stair by stair, to my third-floor locker, to get my jacket and house keys and go home to bed. One stair, rest a bit. Hand, hand, knee, knee, one more stair. Voices in my head argued over me.

"Worthless druggie, can't even climb stairs, you're so blitzed."

"Shut up, asshole. He's fine, no one can tell he's wasted. He'll make it."

"Who do you think you're kidding? It would be the best thing that ever happened to him if he died right here, right now, on these stairs. He probably will."

The locker. I needed to make it to my locker and sit for a while. The stairs, though, they kept going out of focus, turning from white and yellow tiles into swirling tornadoes of colour spiralling toward me, sucking me up, crashing me back down on my hands and knees from a hundred feet in the air. Shattering my forearms, shooting bones through skin, severing my hands at the wrists. Fucking stairs.

Students passed me, going up and down to the next class. No one stopped to ask why I was clawing the staircase, mumbling to myself. Possessed, my eyes rolled back, face drained of colour, mumbling, body separating from mind. Fist clenching reality, slipping, slipping, falling.

"You're dying, Lyndell, just like I told you. Let go. You'll like the other side. Trust me. Let go."

So much gum on the stairs. Why don't they use the garbage?

Lights are bright. Shut my eyes. Nauseous now. My situation slaps me in the face. Each breath gags me, like his cock in my mouth. This is good, puking helps. Move my head, eyes take forever to refocus. Oh God, I'm fucked.

Death seduced me. Grey lit shadows moved over and around me. Squinting against the brightness took more than I had. I relaxed into darkness. My body danced like a marionette on speed. The first seizure consumed me and I jumped, straining, my pelvis shooting toward the ceiling, my head tossing side to side, trying to sever itself from my body. Why did I take a hundred caps of codeine? Fuck, it wasn't supposed to feel like this.

"Just let go and feel how beautiful your departure can be. Stop fighting."

"Hold on, brave boy. You're not going to die. Remember falling off that cliff on your motorbike and splitting your skull? Remember breaking your collarbones and not even crying?"

"I don't want to die. Really, I don't want to die. I don't want to die, I don't want to die."

"Stay awake then. Look at something, anything. Focus. Don't close your eyes."

Tiles rush past, voices yelling, "Open the doors."

"Hurry up, she's going under again."

"Contact the parents."

I tried screaming, " I don't want to see them." Words lost, nothing to focus on, I lie like a corpse.

Tubes hover above me. Beside them a face, deep lines etched around sunken eyes. A dead man, beckoning me to come. Fingers stretched out and curled toward his impatient face.

"What is your problem, child? You've come this far."

Bright lights invaded my eyes. He disappeared, my opportunity with him. Hands gripped my head, tight as a vice. Another pair of hands shoved tubes in my nose. I felt my throat tear. People in white scurried around me. I tried to rip at the tubes, but my arms were secured to the sides of my metal cage. I screamed, "You fucking bastards, I don't want these tubes. It hurts like his penis in my mouth." No response. Blackness.

Fluorescent light attacks me. The walls are padded with foam. Metal sides turn my bed into a cage. It is cold and wet between my legs, where I pissed some time ago. A video camera watches me. "She's awake. Someone get a doctor."

While I was kicking for my life, navigating the channel separating life from death, five days slipped by, unnoticed. Finally, I washed up on shore. Messy, but alive. Voices enter the room, hands prod my weathered body.

"You need to eat, Lyndell. The food cart comes in ten minutes. Be in the dining area."

"You need to take your meds now, Lyndell, you need your meds."

"You need to go to group, Lyndell."

"You need to take a bath."

"You should interact with the other patients, Lyndell."

"No you can't have a shower. No you can't have a razor to shave with."

"No you can't lock the door."

"No you can't talk on the phone."

"No you can't have any visitors."

"No you can't go off the ward."

No. NO. NO.

The piano. It sits still as northern winter in the recreation room, alongside a broken pool table. Posters hang on grimy white cracked walls. Pictures of trees and mountains. The piano is dusty and forgotten. Once-white ivory keys have long since faded to brown and many are missing, exposing gritty wood. There is no bench to sit on, rather a chair with a cracked plastic seat and no back. The piano is badly out of tune. Discordant sound bounces around the room, searching for something to absorb into. I set my hands on the keys and feel roughness beneath my heavy fingertips. I close my eyes and let my fingers wander. It feels like playing teeth on a saw. Without care, the keys will gouge my leaded fingers to a pulpy mess. Gentle. This is the way to touch her. Like touching a baby. Softly, tenderly.

Loud sound ricochets around the room. Notes drift in and out of my head and filter through sterile corridors.

Seated on my leather bench, in front of my grand piano, I spend entire days. TV room, smoke stings my eyes, talk shows, too loud. The cafeteria, supposed to do school work, passed by the medication room to go to bed. Doors locked. People enjoying various stages of numbness. Everyone wants to talk to me. Want me to call them Donald Duck, Rain Man, lend them smokes, have a date in the courtyard. *"Shut up, fuck off, leave me alone."* A needle. Sleep. The morning. The food cart arrives, Sal snatches all the muffins, lines them up in a row, falls to his knees, his hands behind his back. Wailing like a pig in slaughter, slams his face into each muffin, squashing it and banging his head. Bleeding. The nurse, a needle, he sleeps.

Agitated. I try to watch TV, can't sit for more than five minutes. I don't speak. Don't feel human dressed in pink plastic slippers with "Property of Surrey Memorial Hospital" written on them in bold black ink. White robes flap open at the back. I'm cold. I mind my own business. Eat with the nutbars, bump into drug-stiff bodies. Spend time in the bathroom. The door doesn't lock. I forget how to masturbate. No one bothers me. From there to the recreation room. My space, I close the door, separate from chaos. I am furious, frustrated, sick. The piano echoes me. No one interprets the sound. No one asks if I need to talk. The door opens, slams, opens, slams. I ignore it. There will be a needle soon.

The intercom crackles "Medication time." Whatever. My fingers talk back. "Fuck the meds. Get better? That'll never happen in this hell-hole. Your meds are Lucifer in pill form."

A paper cup with pills and one with apple juice appear on the piano. I fucking hate apple juice. I get up, walk to the bathroom, flush the toilet and return empty containers. She gives me more. "Swallow them this time." Open my mouth, thick fingers enter, pull up my tongue, release me. I wait five minutes and puke. Angry, angry.

At the piano again, I sing, pounding fingers up and down and up. *"Telling the truth, just saying how it is. This place sucks, I don't belong here. I am not a puppet. Try and make me a zombie. I dare you. I dare you. I'll kick you in the head, grab the needle from you and shove it up your ass. Ha, ha, ha. You can't touch me. I am not a patient. I'm only here for the free food! Fuckers."* Minor rag-time. Hip-hop blues. Melancholy alternative. Furious classical. Bang bang on the keys. Bleeding fingers a testament to progress.

No psychiatrists, no street clothes, no leaving the ward, no visitors. Only parents. I sit in the smoking room. Mom tells me about morning church service, Dad wrings his hands. I smoke. I am silent. I hate Sundays. They leave. I go back to the piano. Singing again. *"Stand back, fuckers, let my sound out to possess this stinking ward. Let my music gobble up all those pills in the vaulted med room and spew them into the fiery pits of the earth. Light this goddamn hospital on fire from the friction between my fingers and the wooden keys. Watch me laugh as it burns to the ground."*

The paper cups arrive again, a nurse standing over them. I swallow.

enter

the

room

LYNDELL

The greenrooms are always different. sometimes there are none and this becomes a problem because we all need space before a show. i fantasize about all of us having our separate dressing rooms so we could act out our pre-show quirks alone.

Mind you this would never work. i would be knocking on everyone's door asking to come in, not wanting to be alone. i don't know if a show could be a show if i didn't witness zoë trying to copy the rest of a piece onto the page that has the first half printed but then the computer burped and stopped. in an attempt to be organized she is now transferring the remainder of the piece by hand onto the half-printed page, because it would be disruptive to try and flip through four different books on stage to read one story.

except ivan somehow can do that. He can flip through three different books from front to back, and turn a book upside-down because there's one paragraph on a page with a different story, so it was written upside-down to distinguish it from the rest. ivan can also finish writing his stories ten minutes before curtain call. He is relatively calm about all this and I watch in amazement.

I'm so used to hearing anna's voice that if I were in my solitary room, I wouldn't be able to relax. anna chants her lines as though they are a mantra. I suppose they are a mantra, and she wants us all to listen. so I say yes and sit sideways so one ear can listen to her and the other can tune my violin which has already been tuned four times, but we tune because we care and I need to practice because I can't play it _perfectly_ yet, and the show starts in ten minutes, but really, anna, I'm listening.

zoe wonders where her other sock is; anna wants to know if she should ditch this line; ivan's hand moves furiously as though his pen were loaded with rocket fuel. I sit on my milk crate because I have said no to a private dressing room (yeah right!). I play my violin and watch as the scene unfolds. I think what a bunch of fucking freaks we all are, and how ivan got his wish, he's in the circus. And I think about how much I love this, and how if it were any different it wouldn't be the same. Two minutes until curtain. I need to pee, but we're all hugging and getting hyped and saying things I can't remember later and then the lights are up.

Ladies and Gentlemen . . . Taste This.

Skin to Scar

Anna

Look at me. Look carefully. Do you see my face? My totally asymmetrical face? My nose is clinically described as a deviated septum. My mandible and maxilla aren't perfectly lined up, and X-rays show that my chin is connected to my jaw with wire. Yes, I'm a head injury patient and a beautiful one at that. A beautifully built woman—I have the doctors to thank. Six surgeries and ten years of orthodontic treatment later, compliments of the Ontario Medical Plan and the University of Toronto's Faculty of Dentistry. They did a wonderful job, don't you think? My scars are practically invisible. No one would notice unless looking really carefully, and most people don't look really carefully at anything, for fear of offending. Look at me. It's OK. I won't curdle and I certainly won't say I broke my nose playing hockey. I don't want my scars to be invisible. I refuse to disappear into the suffocating folds of feminine mystique and beauty. This face was rebuilt.

＊　　＊　　＊

"OK Anna, I'm going to give you some gas and it's going to relax you. It's going to be OK. You're going to look beautiful. Just beautiful … Are you ready?" the doctor boomed.

"Yeah, I'm ready."

"OK, when I put the mask on your face start counting back from 100. I'll count with you."

"100, 99, 98, 97, 96, 95 …"

I come to several hours later on a stretcher, with my left arm extended up over my head and my right arm and knee bent, in the rescue position. The bright fluorescent lights, corked smell of ammonia, bottled piss, latex powder and anti-bacterial handwash tell me I'm in a hospital. I hate hospitals with a passion. I want to go away, go under again. A nurse is standing over me, just inches away from my face. Her eyes are as big and blue as the moon. Her nose appears disproportionately large, and the rest of her face is out of focus.

"You did really well, Anna. You're going to be OK."

I try to move my flaccid muscles. The room shakes violently as I move my head ever so slightly. I close my eyes again. I have no control over my Demerol-filled body.

"I know you want to move, but you can't. Just relax. Take it slow. Do you hear me?" I blink in response, hoping to quiet her loud words.

"Listen, you can't move because you might vomit and vomiting could be fatal. You need to stay in the rescue position, Anna."

I moan.

"Are you in pain?"

I nod.

"I can't give you any painkillers yet—you need to come out of the anaesthetic first."

I close my eyes in self-defence. *If you can't help me, then why the fuck did you ask me if I'm in pain?* The exhaustion, sweet as blistering summer heat, takes me. I don't have the energy to hang on to my anger. Drift out to a mirage of soft shapes and muted colours. When I come to, my sense of time is adrift. *How long was I gone for? Where did I go?* The lights aren't as bright, the pain is sharper, and I have new accoutrements. There is an IV in my left forearm, a tube is hanging out of my nose—I think it goes into my stomach. A third tube trails between my legs. This one is to piss through. The surgeon appears.

"Congratulations, Anna. The surgery went well, really well. You'll feel better in no time, no time at all. The nurses will take good care of you." He squeezes my shoulder and disappears into the faded brown curtains.

Try to speak, but I can't open my mouth. I want to tell him to keep his hands off of me. I want to ask him why he repeats everything he says twice. And I want to know why everyone keeps telling me I'll be OK. I close my eyes again, digest the fact that this man has just cut me open, moved my jaw around and put me back together again with wire.

The last conversation before the surgery had been a sobering one. The surgeon spoke very matter-of-factly, sounding like a well-practiced and bored lecturer.

"You know, it's a risky surgery. It's kind of like taking apart an Oreo cookie. When you separate the wafers, occasionally they crumble." He grimaced and charged ahead. "We'll also be operating in a very sensitive area. The nerves may not regenerate and in that case, you won't have any sensitivity in your lips or chin. Sometimes it takes the nerves up to two years to regenerate and become functional and you may only regain twenty or forty percent sensitivity. Nerves are touch and go … On the other hand, it could be really smooth and you'll look beautiful, just beautiful."

I imagined a cookie crumbling and pondered the very real possibility of never again being able to feel a lover's lips on mine.

this face was rebuilt

You see, when I say I was rebuilt, I truly mean rebuilt. Bone by bone. Muscle to tendon.

Skin to scar. I couldn't breathe or eat very well prior to all of the surgeries and treatment. Prior. Of course you'd like to know what, where, why, how. Why all of the treatment and surgeries? A fair question and I'd like for that part of my story to be a part of this one. I have, after all, begun a narrative which begs this answer. Why? I don't know why. That answer is buried in the back of the closet with my mother's scorn, my dad's tears and the rest of my family's heavy, well-worn blanket of silence. I can say this: it wasn't a hockey accident.

Layered, sleepy voices echo in patronizing tones. "You'll be beautiful, just beautiful. Beautiful."

Beautiful. Yes beautiful. Sometimes I'm not sure if I actually want the dubious honour of being a beautiful woman. You see, I was not a beautiful girl. I considered beauty an obsession of the weak-minded, and a commodification of life by tight-fisted companies and government. Anyway, I'm not going to carry on with a political rant (and I most certainly could). These words repeat: "Beautiful, you'll be just beautiful. Isn't she beautiful? Oh yes, she's just gorgeous." Sharp, demanding tones.

You know, I couldn't chew food because my jaw was so far out of alignment, and sleep meant feeling my own breath suffocating me. The surgeries were needed for medical reasons—and there were "cosmetic benefits." And this, the cosmetic benefits, is what seemed to excite and intoxicate the doctors more than anything else. I remember the calculated, hungry look in the eyes of surgeons who saw me the way an architect might view a partially constructed building. "Lovely foundation, it's a shame that it's not finished." They saw me as incomplete, unfinished and potentially beautiful. And what greater gift could a doctor give to this world than one more beautiful woman?

I was to them the mythic frog prince, the ragged chimney sweep come Cinderella. I could hold this story close to my breast, hide it, and no one would know. My scars, after all, are quite invisible. According to the tale, the prince never spoke of his former life as a frog and Cinderella never told of her life as a servant. This is part of the supposed magic of the tales. The transformed heroes or heroines are able to assume a new identity, keeping their "secrets" to themselves.

Forsaking a whole life of experience and stories and sweat in exchange for a new life doesn't seem like such a sweet deal to me. But, in all fairness, any deal is an agreement between two parties, and I never made an agreement with anyone to forsake myself and become Cinderella. So, this magical tale is mine to tell, freely, without shame or fear of punishment.

None of the doctors ever asked me how I felt about my face. Go ahead, ask me now … How do I feel? I can say this: I grew these bones myself, muscle to tendon, skin to cheek. I pushed myself into this world and this is magic.

Silent

Lyndell

Sometimes a sound will find its way into the cavern of an ear and remain, to be called upon when a soul is in need of feeding. Sometimes, words carve so deep into the bank of a memory that endless hours of sanding will not fade their mark. Sometimes a touch will reach through the skin and caress the blood beneath. Other times it will curdle it.

Sometimes a smell will linger just inside flared nostrils and tickle on its way, inducing saliva. Sometimes a sight will remain on the inside of closed eyelids, provoking the heart to smile.

Sometimes a voice is muted by the awe of sight. Sometimes a story is told in a stranger's eyes, words unnecessary. Words would only slash open the thin skin of trust. Skin in the fetal stage will not clot and heal leaving only a scar, but bleed until the beat of life beneath the thin sheath of flesh stops and slowly turns grey. And so, silence remains.

Sometimes words, not yet ready to be made audible, find their way through ink blotches on paper to the doorstep of the one who inspired them. To be read silently in the voice of the one who received the carefully folded pages.

Sometimes, meticulously composed and choreographed words need not ears to fall upon, but arms to embrace.

Sometimes words are not required at all. For the silence between a scar and a watchful eye creates resounding sound that finds its way into the cavern of an ear. To remain. To be called upon when a soul is in need of feeding.

Broken Bread

zoë

There was a time he took a piece of her, precious. The kind of taking you can't take back. But today she stands the woman that piece of precious grew into. Her eyes meet you head-on, like truth. She has travelled hard and righteously to this place to see and hold this key. There is a lock on a door in a wall of lies he used to keep her small, when it was time she was growing. She slips the key into that hollow place. Her lips mouth the word, map the journey, open. And now all it takes is just a flick of the wrist and all the courage her stories can summon. She turns the key. As whispers become screaming she sets those secrets free. There is a sound like black crows flying and she sets those secrets free. Lies are not quiet when they're dying, and she sets those secrets free.

And so, living day-to-day across the width of a country from her beginning, she gets a long-distance phone call to tell her that as per standard legal procedure, shame-filled memories have been read aloud by men in uniform in a government building. And now there is a voice, sincere, hoping it is helping. Plastic is what she's holding. Her claims have been validated by a book of laws that has called her dirty for all her history. For the briefest of moments its facts lined up with hers. Old wounds torn open and sewn shut with a sentence, case closed.

He has been found guilty; something that won't fix anything. A stranger's judgement is the only language left between them, they

whose ancestors toiled out a living from a patch of fertile dirt under a burning sun when justice was still served up at the dinner table, bread and silence broken together. Same roots under their feet, same blood around their bones, running as red as the wine at a family meal, red as Communion, nourishing the roots of a family tree that has been twisting through generations, transplanted to rocky Canadian soil and still thriving through her, limbs shifting toward any small bit of sunlight. She rests the plastic in its cradle and speaks aloud to his presence in her memory: "You're gonna die in jail, old man."

The sun slips below the mountains outside her window framed in cracked paint, casting shadows around the room she moves through, making dinner with her hands, skin the colour of her father, a recipe passed down from her mother. She allows herself one slow glance at the bruised sky and the sinking sun as she stirs and lowers the gas flame.

She looks over this week's schedule as she eats and allows her busy life to take over like rush hour, like the tide coming in over rocks and sand. The past being just that and the days full of lists of things to do. In the back of her mind rocky words still spill, half-formed thoughts, waiting for the traffic to clear, waiting for the hand of gravity to pull back the tide and reveal them so she can articulate, touch and feel the ocean floor of her story.

One night as she is undressing for bed she catches her own naked-ness in the mirror above her dresser. It is the first time since before the trial began that she remembers being caught off guard. At first she looks away, too preoccupied to meet the steady gaze of her own reflection, but something draws her eyes back. They follow the full curve of her from the animated spiralling of molasses curls on fire to the most subtle deformation of her smallest toenail. She takes an inventory of the parts that carry her. They have always had a private story, she and her body. Like the way she touched herself when she was little, like the way she touches herself still. No one, not even he, can take everything. This is a good body, a body that has carried her

97

through bad relationships and courtrooms, through sweaty nights in tender arms. She moves in, scrutinizing her face with its soft brush of a smile around full lips, the high and hollow of her cheeks where private tears run wild through barely etched lines of growth that deepen with every experience. There is something I have missed in all of this, she thinks. Somewhere in this crazy mix is cause for celebration.

Late one morning in early spring, with the cherry blossoms budding and the crocuses about to burst, she called me and we talked for a while about how all the meetings and deadlines can dwarf the things that are truly happening in our lives. She said it had been three months since the trial, three months that seemed to have gone by as fast as three days. She invited me to a dinner she was planning.

That Sunday I took extra care with the crease in my dress pants. I buttoned my best dry-clean-only shirt right up to its smart little collar. I adjusted the black belt on my hips just so. I donned my tired old boots polished to a soft but noble shine and walked beside familiar bookstores, game shops and Italian coffeehouses, down past gentrified properties and ramshackle apartments. There was a mist that night and new green life springing up in and around the upstaged asphalt, drinking in the dewy wetness.

When I came to her house my knuckles rapping on old wood seemed like the only sound for miles. The door opened into a room full of familiar faces. She was in the kitchen tending to sauces and bowls full of greens and bright colour. She moved about the counter and the stove, one ear tuned to our voices, adding in, sipping wine and stirring definitions. Below the hum of words and the easy rolling laughter there was the steady base note of cutlery being placed on soft linen.

Steaming pots of perfectly *al dente* pasta and glorious-smelling sauces were carried from the kitchen to the dining room table. When everyone was seated, all glasses were raised to the chef and the feast of sights and smells before us. The conversation petered down to a slow trickle as eating began in earnest.

When it picked up again it had the mellow tone of good company well fed. It flowed through me like the warm smell of bread and garlic filling the room, the way each of us seated there formed a part of the shifting fabric of each other's lives.

The woman who invited us here cleared her throat almost imperceptibly and spoke. "There is a reason I wanted you all to come here tonight," she said. From the corner of my eye, I saw her raise her glass to her lips, swallow and return it to its place on the table. I ached to hold·her, to give her a reassuring caress, my hand placed lightly on hers. Something, anything to convince myself as much as her that things are OK. But some things aren't OK. Some things never will be. Some things are valuable simply for being a part of us, because we have survived them. That is why nothing, not even a caress, must distract her. When she raises her eyes again the words around the table recede to make room. Into that vessel of silence she pours the words of her story.

Quick Fix
Ivan

I was a lot of things when I was a kid—a lot of things was I—a pirate, a pauper, a cowboy, a king, but when it came to being a girl, I choked, I stumbled, I dropped my sword, struck out.

There was a time when I tried being—if not truly wanting to be—a good little girl. I went through a stage where I tried to wear a dress, keep my knees clean, be seen and not heard, cross my legs and hope to die. I did try.

Too many times stewing over the inevitable grass stain, the sticky discomfort of satiny underpants, the unbearable tightness of being dressed like a lady, left me folded up inside at the humiliation of it all. Inevitably I was informed that even in chiffon and pumps I still walked like a tomboy, that my shoulders were too muscly for a strapless and my tits too small for a push-up bra. I forgot that you can't do karate kicks in a long dress and landed on my ass. *If you only tried just a little harder, it's just this once, just for the wedding. Come on out, it's just me and the shop lady here, sweetheart, I'm sure you look just lovely.*

I remember the day I found my little sister's tampons. Being the tomboy late-bloomer that I was, I didn't hang with a lot of girlie-girls, they made me feel awkward, incomplete somehow, under-dressed. Dirty, even.

I asked her what they were.

Tampons, retard, whaddaya think they are, pontoons? They're for when you're on the rag. What? You mean you haven't got yours yet? Had mine for about two years now.

She was fifteen, two years younger than I. I didn't realize at the time what a big deal it was gonna be that I was not to bleed until I was almost nineteen years old. By the time I did, no one, not the doctors, not my mom, neither of my grandmothers—both of whom seemed unnaturally concerned with my progress in this department—and certainly not I, believed that I was even capable of it.

By that time *she's a late bloomer, nothing to worry about,* had turned into *she's too skinny, she runs too much, plays hockey too much,* had turned into *let's just run a few little tests, just to see what we might be dealing with here, just to see what we can . . . rule out.*

To the young me, menstruating was no more or less elusive than say cleavage or curling irons; that is, it was just one more thing that real girls seemed to have a natural grip on, that I vaguely didn't.

Then it was decided by my mother and the doctor who birthed me—the very same one who slapped my ass first, had a quick peek and then proclaimed whether it was to be shop class or home-ec for me—that a little extra estrogen would fix me right up, give me some pubic hair to hide that dangling clit, and who knows, maybe that unsightly hair around my nipples would give it up and fall out, too.

It worked, I guess, in a way, for in a couple of months on a hockey-practice Sunday morning I sat down on the toilet and there she be—blood between my too-white thighs and sweat on my upper lip.

The pills had worked.

Figures, I thought at the time, that the very same guy who fucked this whole thing up in the first place has had to cover his ass in these times of malpractice suits and such, and I come out the loser, me with hockey practice and cramps and being eighteen years old and having not a fucking clue what to do about it. My parents had never told me, you see, and I wasn't about to press my little sister for the gory details.

My parents, in their own unwitting way, were part of the source of my gender euphoria. On this day my mom was out of town on business and my dad was downstairs cooking crêpes and drinking Scotch with my Uncle Ed. Ed, whom the whole family has felt slightly estranged from ever since he was ratted out by a righteous biker and arrested by a rookie cop on Main Street in Whitehorse. He was charged with indecent exposure after the same overzealous flatfoot dragged him out of his truck from under a faded cotton army blanket, pants down, dick in hand, a shocked and empty stare ringing in his blue eyes from under his greying red hair.

He was acquitted after the guy who he fixes heavy equipment for wrote him a character reference on company stationery. He has six kids, after all, and a wife from New Zealand who talks through her nose and embarrasses him in public with talk of colonic enemas. She makes him eat orange juice on his cornflakes because she's dead against dairy this week. The poor man is stressed out, and so poor Uncle Ed, the quiet one, disappeared into the bush to work until the worst of it blew over, and he just got back into town, and so Dad's having him over for a belt and a crêpe and I'm having my period.

"Dad? Cuddya come here for a sec?"

"Whaddaya want? I'm burning my crêpes already!"

"It's, uhh, kinda private, you know. Think you could maybe just come up here for a minute, please?"

"'Sjust me and yer Uncle Ed here, what the hell do you want?"

"Please, please, please just come here …"

"Oh for fuck's sake," and he is standing in the bathroom door, out of breath from taking the stairs three at a time. "What is it?"

"I'm bleeding—"

"What?" he cut me off. "Didya fall down, didya slip? What, are you OK?"

"No. Well … I mean yes … I mean, I'm bleeding … you know, it's like, I got my period."

The resulting physical reaction on my father's part I can only attempt to describe in the following fashion: everything moved, except his feet, and his brain. His hands moved in a cross between a wave and a shake, his head said yes and no at the same time. Finally he got his breath and spoke. "Don't move," he stammered, letting all his air out with just these two words, looking vaguely fearful. Of me? Of blood? Of women in general? I could not tell you, and if I were to ask him about it now, I'm sure his mind has forgiven him by forgetting the whole incident altogether.

"I'll getcha something from your mother's bathroom."

It was technically both their bathroom, situated mere feet from the bed they both slept in, but compact and clean and smelling only of her, full of she-things, it was reverently referred to by all of us as "my mother's bathroom." These things seemed insignificant then, not so much so now.

He returned moments later with a crumpled cardboard box. He still didn't quite have control over his extremities, but he could now formulate a sentence.

"Should be instructions in the box. I ... I mean, I hope you're ... I hope you're feeling ... better, uhh, soon." He retreated, backpedalling so as to not turn his back to me, and I was alone again, just me and the box that lay on the floor at my feet, smack in the middle of the fuzzy blue bath mat that matched the towels and the little hand soaps we never touched because they were matching.

I pulled out the instructions and studied them with some confusion at first. You see, in his panicked state my father had grabbed the first box his hand felt in the drawer in my mother's bathroom, and in his rush to help me out he had innocently presented me with a box of scented anal suppositories.

Poor man. He was never much good in a crisis. He is also short-tempered and always says the wrong thing at funerals.

I sighed like only a daughter can at her father's shortcomings, and waddled, pants down, across the hall. I dragged the phone into my room and called my grandmother. "Hey Pat," I said. She always liked for us to call her Pat; Grandma made her feel too old, she said.

"Hello-o there, de-ar," came her voice back through the receiver. Comfort incarnate she was, is and always will be to me.

"Hey, I got my period—"

"Congratulations!" she cut me off, sounding thrilled.

I wasn't.

"Yeah, whatever, but look, I have hockey at two o'clock and my mom is out of town and Dad is drunk downstairs with Ed and he can't cope at all, and I don't have anything here and he just gave me a box of ... scented anal suppositories."

"Who did, Ed did?"

"No, no ... my dad did. He's one of your other sons."

My grandmother doesn't really laugh aloud, she kind of just lets air out through her nose in a bemused fashion. It was this sound I heard next, and then these kind words: "He always was a little thick, your father. Poor man. He can't help himself. These things frighten him terribly, you know. Put a little tissue in your panties and come on over, dear. I'll take you to the Super-A and we'll fix you right up with what you'll need. Then we can come back home and you and I can have a wee drink to celebrate. Congratulations, you are a woman now. A full-grown woman."

Her voice sounded like I should be proud of myself, so I humoured her and got off the phone. I love my grandmother almost more than anyone in this world, and I needed her comfort right then along with her humour, her sharp wit and her blackcurrant tea and scones with honey.

Walking the four blocks from my parents' house to hers, I thought it all over, kicking stones and pulling leaves from trees on the path, taking longer than I needed to, dilly-dallying as she would call it. She always had tea on and advice to give to all of us, fourteen uncles, twelve aunts and thirty-six cousins. She might run out of milk at times, but she never came up short for an opinion.

I knew there was more to my future womanhood than this. My mother, my grandmothers, and maybe even the doctor just wanted for everything to be OK for me. For me to bleed, thus marry, thus bear children and be happy (like they were?). By the only standards they knew, bleeding was in my best interests, and bleeding I finally

had worked

was, so they were all happy for me. Pleased with me for finally performing the most involuntary task I ever engaged in.

I had always known that this small town and a husband and kids were not to be my destiny, and in retrospect, at least, they must have seen it too. I was never a good little girl, and even at the tender age of eighteen, I was an old hack when it came to other people's gender confusion with regard to myself.

But my father's mother had never given me any flak about wearing a dress or minding my manners or crossing my legs. She had always told me just to be who I was, do what I liked, that I could be whatever I wanted to be when I grew up, that the world was changing. She holds more than her share of the world's wisdom, and has always held and spouted complex theories regarding men and their ways, and the ways women cope and survive and raise up the little ones and make ends meet in spite of them. And now the first feminist I ever knew was patting my back for bleeding and ushering me into my womanhood with a Scotch 'n' soda.

That afternoon she lifted up her flowered print dress and showed me how to put a tampon in, cursing my mother and Catholics and closed-minded people for not teaching me this already. She stroked my head and cooked me lunch and gave me kind advice and stain removal hints, but she did not have the answers I really needed that day.

She had successfully raised up four sons, and I was her first grandchild, her first boy-girl, and she being a high femme in her heyday, she could not help me with this one.

I knew then but did not say it, not aloud, anyway, that if there were indeed answers out there for all the questions circling in my heart, that I was going to have to ask and answer them for myself.

IVAN

Little known fact: Anna and I were lovers, for a while, years ago. I wooed her in a bookstore one day by reading _The Cat in the Hat_ aloud to her in an overtly sexual fashion, as though it were sticky hand pornography. It was just perverted enough that she noticed me.

It wasn't a particularly lengthy or successful affair, and I would have to shoulder most of the responsibility for that. The timing was all wrong, you see. I was too young and unpolished to withstand prolonged exposure to a femme of her depth and magnitude.

Anna was, even back then, all woman, all backbone and she-blood and beauty. And I—I didn't know enough about who I was yet to realize that I couldn't compete, that I shouldn't compete, because I was an apple, and she was ... a peach.

I had not embraced the in-between that I was. Anna knew

that there was a handsome lad inside of me, but all I knew was that I was not beautiful.

To me, she was haute cuisine, and next to her I felt like the no-name brand, like the stuff in the bright yellow box with the square black letters. I still felt like an accomplice whenever a stranger called me sir, complicit somehow in man crimes I could not really commit. Back then, I had words for what I wasn't, but none for what I was. I didn't know how to spell me.

I watch her now, how her love for Lyndell swells in her chest and shines behind her eyes. she loves the she-in-him, and the he-in-her, and Lyndell is rounder and taller because of it. This is spoken aloud and acknowledged, but still magic.

sometimes, it takes a woman just like her to love boys like us.

we are all backstage at the Lotus. It is ten minutes before show time. Lyndell is tuning his violin, zoë has lost something vital but is trying not to let her panic disturb others. I have decided all of a sudden that I don't want breasts on-stage tonight, and Anna, by now a master of the fine art of binding boy tits, is helping me.

I am naked from the waist up, and she wraps the tensor bandage around my chest, tenderly but tight. Her hands are not as soft as they look. I do up my buttons, she adjusts my collar and smooths down the flat white front of my dress shirt for me. she has one hand on each of my shoulders. There is blood and water and time between us. she tells me I am handsome, and I believe her.

bent

Border Crossing: Cop a Feel

z o ë

Pulled over, wouldn't you fucking know it and so close to home. I was ready for it going down to Seattle for this show for which you could say we have no permit and therefore no legal right to collect American money for our talents. But now, coming home, I can practically feel my hot little shower cubicle and my warm blankets surrounding me. The four of us straightening out the last-minute details. What equipment needs to go back where, to whom, by when, doling out the chores and going home.

We've earned our rest. I'll order in, I'll curl up under my nice warm Canadian blankets with a good book. Right now, I'm freezing cold. I can't remember how we got here, what series of questions led to us being pulled over in this mid-border parking lot limbo. Do we know for sure this car is clean and up to snuff? I don't know anything about cars. I've never owned one. I've never owned a computer either. I'm beginning to see the merits of saving things on disk. All my writing is neatly—well, my version of neatly—stored between the covers of a black bound hardcover book that cost ten dollars and serves as my journal.

Three border cops wearing latex gloves are going over the contents of our trunk. We prepared for this. We talked about it. We are so squeaky clean, surely there's nothing they could take us in for. So why am I nervous? The worst thing they could do to me would be to read my journal out loud. I hope my friends and colleagues would

112

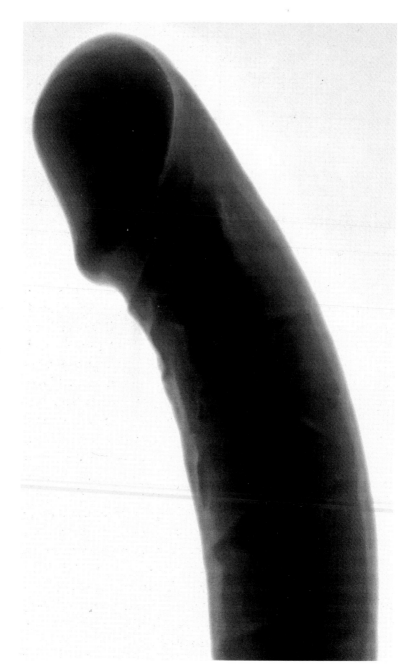

have the decency to cover their ears. There are no clever stashes between those covers, no blotters of acid stuck between the pages. I checked, twice.

Anna is wearing a kilt. Goosebumps are beginning to rise on her lovely Mediterranean legs. She whispers to the three of us standing apart from the inspectors, "I'm not wearing any underwear." At any other time in any other place this would be an amusing playfully mischievous revelation. Was this some sort of arrangement between her and Lyndell? Has the honeymoon stage seriously impaired her judgement or did she just think it would be fun to cross a major international boundary with more layers protecting her feet than her cunt and her ass. What exactly do these bored self-important motherfuckers need to have for an excuse before they put us in separate rooms and tell us to spread wide, real wide.

I watch these guys pawing over our possessions. Lyndell's violin with its decades of history, its melodious hymns and songs of rebellion and survival almost sings out when they touch its strings, but it knows better and makes only a soft muffled plunk of g-string sound. Pages of scrawled writing, words of remorseless sexual pride and celebration, confusion, courage and identity are in their hands. I know that when it comes to men in uniform with guns on their hips, these things are a punishable offence. Confusing these guys is a crime. Being proud of the things about yourself that confuse them makes it worse. To cross the U.S./Canada border without incident it is best to look and act as though you never have and never would think of crossing any border, metaphoric or otherwise, without the express permission of someone very official with a government-issued badge and uniform. Either that or you yourself have to actually own the border outright. If you do not own it, transgressions are not allowed.

Watching their gloved hands, I try to make myself and all my friends, colleagues and lovers disappear. If they don't see us they can pretend we don't exist and save themselves the trouble of being offended. Their latex gloves cause me to reflect on how many different implications latex gloves can have.

Ivan lights a smoke, trying to stay cool, trying to keep warm. Anna shifts her weight slowly from one foot to the other. She does her best to control Lyndell's darting aggravated eyes with her own. The border cops are burrowing into Lyndell's suitcase. They have just finished frisking her violin. None of us would ever touch Lyndell's violin without her permission. Mostly out of respect but also because we know better. You just don't go there. Invasion being a matter of degrees, we breathe a sigh of relief when they leave her violin alone and begin to rifle through her bag. She watches them intently for a moment, Anna urging her quietly to relax. Lyndell breaks her steady gaze on the trunk and turns to us with a sly little grin on her face.

"He's feeling my dick," she says reflectively, as if wondering which boxers she put on under her jeans this morning.

Stretched
Lyndell

115

If I had no tits, it wouldn't be much different than it is now. I mean, people don't see my tits under baggy T-shirts and slouched shoulders. They are well hidden, tucked under layers like painful truth. The difference would lie in two extra inches of pride. I would show off my scars, mounted on my chest like a medal of valour. Yeah, if I had no tits, I would be taller.

Just Like My Dad

Ivan

I was lying on his bed, watching him button his black jeans. His pressed white shirt, black belt and black leather vest were all laid out, ready for him to slide into. The equivalent of dress blues for a lesbian. He used to be a lesbian.

"I don't miss them a bit, not a bit." His voice was warm honey rolling over gravel, and his small-for-the-rest-of-him hands kept returning to the still-angry scars on his chest, like a tongue to a missing tooth.

He stands taller, since his breasts were removed, because his honey-gravel voice and sparse mustache now match the rest of him.

"Look at you," he rumbled, so I looked down at my stretched-out self. "You're built like a teenage boy that grew tits by accident. And you're too thin. We'll have to fatten you up."

He grins and then bares one of his eye teeth at me, a friendly predator. His shirt is buttoned up, belt buckled, vest on, he is ready to take that girl out for dinner. He kisses the top of my head and is gone, just the smell of him is left in the room with me.

I have known him for five years, and he is my surrogate father, my queer dad, the head of my freak family. He calls me his son, and I am proud of this. He was already my dad back when he was a she.

I can't explain this, so I'll just use words:

Sometimes, I want to be just like my dad when I grow up, but without the scars.

Drag Race
zoë

Tim stood in a crowd as thick as the stale cigarette smoke that surrounded them, taking drink orders from four German guys. They asked her what was the best way to meet women in Rodhos and she said, "Just be your charming selves." They asked her what she was doing later. She pretended not to hear and pushed her way into the crowd, letting the loud music and the wall-to-wall people swallow her up. Very tactfully handled, she thought. Great, she'd be evading their passes for the rest of the night. She'd have to stay nice, though. Waitresses at Sweet Dollies were all illegal and highly expendable.

The band ran onto the stage and launched into "Hotel California" amidst cheers and applause. Taking orders near the stage was almost impossible. When the band was playing she was as likely to get crushed as she was to find a customer. There were three bars in Sweet Dollies. She'd been stuck at the middle bar to tough it out near the dance floor. "Can I get you anything?" Tim shouted as politely as she could at a young Greek guy she was sure she hadn't asked before. He gave her a sideways glance and dismissed her with a wave of his hand.

Tim squeezed her way toward the bar, past unidentifiable limbs, full drinks and white teeth and eyes glowing in the black light, convulsing under the occasional strobe. When the bartender caught sight of her, she motioned for her to come quickly and pointed to the telephone that was resting on the bar. It had to be Daina. No one else would call her here. She made her way as quickly as she could and

117

reached the bar out of breath. Inger handed her the phone and said, "Don't look now but Yannis is watching from the balcony. If he asks you what you were doing on the phone later tell him it was your mother calling to see how you were. For some reason that seems to wash with him."

"OK," said Tim. She took a deep breath and prepared to sound calm. "Hello Daina."

"Tim," came the voice from half a continent away, "how the hell are you?"

"Much better now," said Tim. "I can't talk for long but it's great to hear your voice."

"You too," said Daina. "I guess I better get straight to the point then. Is it expensive to rent dirt bikes there?"

"Not bad, why?"

" 'Cause I keep having this dream of drag-racing you on a dirt road in Greece and then jumping in the sea naked."

"Excuse me?" said Tim. "Daina, are you saying you have the money to come to Greece?"

"It would take me another month or so but I figure I could swing it for say three or four weeks. Would that work for you?"

"Uh, yeah, that would definitely work for me. Except that I think riding a dirt bike naked would be painful."

"Yeah, especially since you'll be eating my dust."

"Come here and say that."

"Careful what you wish for," said Daina. "I'll call you again soon, OK?"

"OK," said Tim. She handed the phone back to Inger.

"That grin oughtta earn you a few tips," said Inger.

"Yeah," said Tim, "but if I hear 'Hey baby' one more time I think I'm gonna sock someone."

"Sounds good for the soul but bad for business," said Inger. Her short blond hair was gelled sleek and smooth. Her lips coated in crimson floated in the bar light. She was making five different drinks as she spoke.

Two weeks later at the end of the night Tim sat at the bar with the other waitresses subtracting her drink totals from her float. One thousand drachma in tips. Good, not great but good. Maybe this would be worth it after all. One more month of tips like this and she might have enough to go island-hopping with Daina. When all the waitresses finished their addition they made their way up the balcony stairs to Yannis's office to settle their evening's accounts with him.

Tim couldn't remember them ever agreeing that going to his office together would be the ritual, but she figured they all felt just that much better about walking into Yannis's office with five more women behind them. Whenever Tim made her way up these stairs little nursery rhymes came to her. "The king is in his counting house ..." she hummed to herself as she mounted the heavily varnished wooden steps. What a fortune it must have cost to build this place, huge as it was and all in English pub style with thick wooden beams. And there was enough electricity pumping through it to fuel a huge sound system and keep the entire place air-conditioned from dusk till dawn.

They reached the balcony at the top of the stairs and headed to the back. She always felt like she was in a spy movie when she went to Yannis's office. It was well hidden, strategically placed to avoid enquiring tax police whose laws he routinely "overlooked."

Yannis himself looked like a cross between The Godfather and Bozo the Clown. He had a wonderful smile that made the two tufts of hair left on either side of his head stand at attention. When he smiled like that, she could almost imagine him as a child, but she tried not to since she could never be sure his smiles were sincere.

He sat behind a heavy schoolteacher's desk and was always surrounded by plastic shopping bags full of bills in various denominations. Each waitress told him her drink totals, handed him a stack of bills and drink receipts and waited while he counted first the receipts and then the money. If the total was correct he nodded and moved on to the next. When all this was done they rose to go and left him to his accounting.

Tim was just about to follow the rest of the women out the door when Yannis turned to her and said, "Sit, sit. I want to talk with you." The last woman out the door gave Tim a sympathetic look as she disappeared through the one-way mirror and was gone. Yannis looked up momentarily from his counting, gave Tim a quick smile and said, "Close the door, please." He wrote a final figure down, turned to her and said, "Yes, it's about the pants."

"The pants?"

"Yes, for three weeks now I have been hoping you will change them, but every day it's the same thing. I think maybe you wash them every day."

"Actually, I have more than one pair."

He sighed. "Look, you are a nice girl, a pretty girl, attractive, but every day you wear these same pants. They are so big for you, you look like a truck driver. It's not good for business. I'm not sure, I think maybe you lost a lot of weight or something." He smiled. Perhaps this last remark was meant to be a compliment.

Tim felt herself paste on something that she hoped looked like a smile and thought, I need this job, I need this job, I need this job.

"I hope I don't insult you," Yannis said. He laughed, she laughed, they pretended they were laughing together.

The next week Tim appeared in clothes a lot like the ones she usually wore, only ten sizes smaller. They were uncomfortable, to say the least. Inger thought she looked so sad that she offered to buy her a coffee at the Paradise after work.

"I don't know, Inger," said Tim. "I really don't know if I can do this. I'm so uncomfortable. I just don't know how to wear all this tight, sexy stuff and feel good in it." She looked disparagingly down at her tight blue jeans and too-small T-shirt. "My drink sales have dropped this week, tips have been nonexistent or so insulting I want to throw them back in their faces. I'm outta my element, man." Tim cuddled a latte, took deep pulls on her smoke and glanced out of the open-air café over rooftops and palm trees at a fuchsia-coloured sunrise.

"Poor Tim," said Inger. "Beaten by a hemline and forced to go home early."

"Come on, Inger," said Tim, "give me a break here. I'm serious. This sexy-with-attitude stuff just doesn't come naturally to some of us."

"Look," said Inger, "there is not a woman alive who is not as sexy as all get-out in tight clothes with low hemlines, as long as that woman knows it."

"Unless that woman tends to feel sexiest in hockey gear," said Tim.

"So be that extreme," said Inger. "Look, what you need is to go more than halfway. If you're gonna do this thing, do it straight over the top."

"What, like Olivia Newton John in *Greased Lightning*?"

"Oh yes, girl, just like that."

"But I'm not any little miss Sandra D. I don't need to be transformed."

"Yeah, but you do want tips and the way you're carrying yourself right now, you're apologizing for your very existence. Sandra D. died in that last scene, my friend, and Olivia took full control."

"Inger," said Tim, "are you sure you're not a drag queen disguised as a woman?"

"And what if I am?"

"Then will you dress me?"

"Girl, nothing would make me happier. Want to borrow my black leather thigh-highs?"

"Sure, why the hell not? Oh, and one more thing. When Daina shows up and discovers I've had a sex change, do you think you could help me explain all this to her?"

Two weeks after Tim's make-over she stood in her shoebox-sized one-room apartment donning her new femme fatale work armour. It was a humid Friday night, which would make it Thursday afternoon pick-up hockey time back home at the East Van arena. Daina would at this very moment be sitting on a heavily initialled bench in a grey change room adjusting her well-worn jersey. The Zamboni would be circling the rink, watering and brushing until it was polished to a scratchless smooth surface. Daina had real hockey pants with all the right padding left over from her junior league days.

Tim put on Inger's black leather thigh-highs and wound black laces around brass rivets with fingernails painted in a shade called Blackberry Sin. She imagined Daina's long landscaper's hands, nails chewed short, pulling her skate laces tight. Black nylon and dark leather on top of flashing blades sharpened to carve the traces of her body's movements on the ice. Tim was one of the few people who could keep up with Daina on skates. They were never allowed to play on the same team. They would race each other down the ice for the puck and never let each other rest for even a second without regretting it.

Tim didn't know Daina when she first started playing there but after her first few games she wanted to. She was unsure of Daina, though. Maybe she was one of those all-too-common butches who only dug femmes, at least in public. It was over a month before they did anything but body-check each other in full uniform. But then there was that day they played neck 'n' neck all afternoon. Tim's team won 3 to 2 in the final period. Daina's defense was impenetrable until Tim caught an exceptionally good pass and squeaked the puck past her in the last five minutes. When Daina shook her hand in the post-game line-up her breath was fast and her handshake firm. Daina grinned big, shook her head for a moment and then held Tim's eyes with hers until Tim was almost knocked over by the next player in line taking her hand.

Tim took her time undressing in the change room afterward and spent a full three minutes adjusting the shower temperature even though the water was always lukewarm. Daina didn't seem to be in any hurry either. By the time she wandered lazily into the showers, Tim was already soaping up and the rest of the players were outside deciding where to go for a beer. They showered in silence for a while.

"Tired?" asked Daina.

"Hell no," said Tim. "I could play a whole other game."

"Could you now?" said Daina, eyebrows raised. The water against Daina's forearms and torso made the blood there rise to the surface. Her muscles were still coiled tight from the game. She didn't look like she'd do too badly at another round herself. Daina caught Tim looking at her and grinned. Tim grinned back and the next thing she knew she was slammed up against the tile wall, Daina's hands had her wrists pinned above her shoulders and she was coaxing and teasing Tim's lips with her own. Tim let her work for a moment and then relented, opened her lips and kissed Daina full and deep.

When Daina pulled back Tim caught her breath. "Not one for small talk, are you?"

Daina laughed low. "If it's subtlety you're talking about, you could use a little work yourself."

"I tend to know what I want," said Tim.

"So tell me, what would you like right now?"

"I would like you to bite and tease my nipples; then I would like you to pretend that I have a cock and suck me until I am as hard as a rock and then I would like you to fuck me."

"Jesus, it's nice you know what you want, but it sure took you long enough to ask."

Now Tim sighed as she put on her lipstick. She glanced at her watch, put her feet up on the desk and masturbated. When she opened her eyes, her own flushed reflection—lips a deep, browny purple to match her fingernails—was there in the mirror and she had to admit it was kinda sexy. Inger had done a good job. She seemed to know instinctively what would look good on Tim. Black stretch pants, high boots and sporty snug-fitting shirts. Just different enough from her everyday self to give her a character to play, one she was becoming rather fond of. She dished out attitude with every drink. It was good for a laugh, if nothing else, and her tips had improved. So had her customers' manners. For better or for worse they seemed to understand "look but don't touch" better when she had black leather thigh-highs on. She glanced at her watch again. Shit! Five minutes to make the ten-minute walk to work.

Three hours later Daina stood outside Sweet Dollies Pub and glanced at her watch. Almost midnight. She had made good time from the airport. It had been only two weeks since she last spoke to Tim, but when Daina saw the cheap flights advertised in last week's newspaper she figured she might as well go now as two weeks later. Tim would be so surprised. She glanced up at the sign. This had to be it. How many bars called Sweet Dollies could there be on one island?

Daina walked in the double glass doors and ran straight into the bouncer. "Can I help you?" His voice was as big as his biceps. He had a slightly confused expression underneath his blank bouncer mask. He was trying to place her. His body language said "Well, it takes all kinds and I can beat the shit out of all of 'em." Where her head stopped his shoulders began. God, she hated bars like this. Tim did too; she must be going crazy here. "Uh, yeah, I'm Tim's friend. I'm here to see her, from Canada." She added the word Canada as an afterthought, hoping it would make a difference somehow; knowing that it wouldn't.

"Wait here, please." He shouted something in Greek to a young guy in a Sweet Dollies T-shirt who nodded and disappeared into the crowd.

Then Tim was rushing toward her, throwing her arms around her in a great bear hug and covering her face in highly traceable kisses. Daina laughed nervously and blushed as the doorman looked on in bemusement.

"God, it's good to see you," Tim said, pulling back so she could get a good look at her.

"You too," said Daina, which was true, and was also all she could think of to say. Then she said, "Nice outfit." She wasn't quite sure why she said it that way, as though she didn't fully mean it, as though Tim owed her an explanation.

Tim brushed it away with a laugh. "Yeah, well, you do what you gotta do, eh?

Maybe, thought Daina, and then she felt awful. She'd just been covered in kisses by a woman she'd missed for six months. "You look great. It's just a little different, that's all."

"You must be tired," Tim said. "You could probably use a nap. You wanna have a beer first? It's on the house. There's some people here that would really like to meet you."

Daina was not really in the mood for socializing but what the hell. If it would make Tim happy, one beer wouldn't kill her. Soon she was being introduced to all three bartenders, four waitresses, the bass player and the Dolly Parton clone who fronted the band, who when she wasn't singing smoked profusely and whispered with an English accent. "The voice, darling, my chords are simply killing me, give us a hot toddy, love." Tim hovered around the periphery and floated in and out of the crowd with trays full of drinks. She stopped every once in a while to say hello and then disappeared again.

Daina liked Tim's friends well enough. They all seemed amiable **125** and hetero and happy to meet her. They shook her hand with know- ing smiles and said, "I've heard a lot about you." Daina felt sure they had to practice immense restraint not to nudge her in the side, wink from behind their beers and say, "Yeah, she told me, I'm hip, I'm cool with it. Bet she's a hard one to handle, eh?" Oh Christ, thought Daina, this is too much. I haven't felt this misinterpreted since before I came out, when my straight friends were setting me up with all the nicest guys they knew.

When Stomatese, the bass player, offered to buy her a third beer and later started cracking jokes like what's the difference between a French ho and an English one, it made about as much sense to Daina as anything else that was going on around her.

Daina woke up under a thin sheet on a stone floor in a room the size of a matchbox. Sunlight poured relentlessly through the frosted win- dow. Tim was curled up on a double bed not two feet away. Daina's

126

mouth felt as though she had snacked on fresh Greek beach sand just before bed and forgot to spit it out. Her head was an echo chamber, reverberating what seemed to be a thousand children playing kickball just outside the door. She touched her head delicately, searching for the off switch.

At least she had made it to the right apartment. That would be Tim's doing. Waking up on the floor would also be Tim's doing. Not a good sign when there was a perfectly comfortable double bed two feet away with only one person in it. Waking up on the floor had certain implications that did nothing to help the slightly ill feeling in Daina's stomach. Tim was awake now. Daina could tell. She was awake and pretending not to be. Daina's sense of foreboding grew.

"Tim, I know was a pain-in-the-ass last night. I guess I was just a little overwhelmed, that's all. I was a little jet-lagged and tired and not fully prepared for the straightness of this scene and your get-up, well, it took me by surprise, that's all, and you could jump in any time."

"You were a total fucking asshole," said Tim. "You slapped my ass, you tipped me down my pants. You acted like the worst jerk I've had to put in his place over the past two months."

It sounded so awful when Tim said it that way. Mostly Daina remembered laughing it up with the bass player and then later on the drummer. She remembered how bizarre the whole thing felt but after three beers it all just kinda made her laugh. The three of them checking out the women in the bar together, deciding which ones were tens. It wasn't her fault that Tim came by just then. But then again it wasn't Tim's fault either. Tim was right; she had been a jerk.

Daina knew she was in for some major apologizing. Well, she thought, at least I don't fuck up halfway. I mean, it's not like I have to sit around baiting and dodging and wondering if I might be able to get away with being defensive about the whole thing. The game of kickball continued outside the door: children's voices, peals of laughter and the occasional loud bang as the ball hit the door. In the midst of that mayhem Daina composed her best, her clearest most straightforward apology. "Tim, I'm sorry."

Tim's face softened a bit but the hurt look did not leave her eyes and her body remained tight. "I'm not sure that's good enough. Why did you do that? Is it all about clothing and lipstick? Am I someone you can treat differently when I wear make-up?"

Now Daina felt again like she did last night, like someone pulled the rug out from under her, changed the rules, maybe even the game, and forgot to let her know. "It's about more than that and you know it," she said.

"Yeah, it's about being 'hey babied' and having my ass pinched by strangers until I finally stopped cringing and started flaunting, saying, 'Here's what you want, boys, touch it and you die.' They seem to understand that. Maybe they even enjoy it. Maybe I even enjoy it. It beats the hell out of shitty tips and pretending that it's not happening. You know if any of my customers pulled the shit you did last night I'd nail them to the fucking wall."

"Oh for Christ's sake, Tim," said Daina. "I'm not one of your customers. Last I knew I was your lover. Remember how we used to joke about that? How even the queers couldn't figure us out? Remember how we could talk about things we couldn't get anyone else to understand? Well, I guess there were a few things you forgot to tell me the last time I phoned. So I thought I might have some idea of who it was I was going to see after six months of missing you. I'm sorry if I didn't get it all right away and just rise to the occasion, but it was a little shocking and I'm sorry I acted like a jerk. I'm sorry, I'm sorry, I'm sorry. I mean, what, what else can I say?"

Outside, two kickball goals were scored on the front door while Tim made up her mind. "It was just shitty, that's all," she said finally. "But I guess four apologies and a hangover oughtta count for something. So you wanna see Greece with me or what?"

"Yeah," said Daina.

"I know a sweet little swimming hole down a dirt road at the back of the island. How about we go look into the cost of renting some dirt bikes?"

"Sounds good."

"All right, then," said Tim, "just let me get some clothes on."

Daina dragged herself into the shower, then slipped into a clean pair of jeans and a fresh T-shirt and felt almost human again. When she came out Tim was dressed in a body-tight long-sleeved T-shirt and tight pants, and had her boots on. Her lips had a fresh coat of lipstick.

"Uh, hon," said Daina, "do you have to go to work soon or something?"

"No, it's my week to come in late."

"Well, umm, do you really think that's the right gear to go drag-racing in?"

"I don't see why not."

"Well, it's just that you have lipstick on, and I don't really see the point."

"I just feel like wearing it. Do you have a problem with that?"

"It's just stupid, that's all. I mean, it's just going to come off in five minutes anyway."

"What exactly is your point?" asked Tim. "I can't go drag racing with you if I have lipstick on?"

"Christ, do you have to be so fucking difficult? It's just not practical, that's all."

"I can't believe that you're so shallow that it matters to you whether or not I wear lipstick when I ride a motorbike. Maybe you should find someone else to rent motorbikes with."

"Maybe I should," said Daina, " 'cause I don't know who the fuck you are in that get-up."

"I'm the same person I always was and I can still out-race your ass on a dirt bike in stilettoes with one hand tied behind my back."

Daina finished dressing in silence, opened the door. "Let's see how you do in lipstick first."

Super Hero

anna

The things a girl shouldn't think late at night, I was thinking. Furious, pounding, screaming inside. Thinking the kinds of things a nice girl wouldn't. And yeah, I know, mean and nasty thoughts aren't going help me get to sleep, but tonight I can't just do some deep breathing and hope to crash before the sun rises.

No, tonight is different. Tonight I'm going to close my eyes and think up something really sweet. Something worth missing sleep over.

So there I was walking to Hastings and Commercial after working the four-to-midnight shift. Standing at the streetcar stop for about five minutes, during which time drive-by assholes call me sugar, baby, bitch, honey, cunt, cocksucker ... You get the picture. I feel like a sitting plastic duck that gets pelted at the fair. If you hit the duck three times out of four you win yourself an ugly pink-and-white stuffed rabbit. Almost no one really wants a stuffed rabbit. We want what it means: a prize, trophy, medal. We like to win, and we like proof.

I decide to walk, dragging my feet. A van pulls up alongside me, passenger window already conveniently rolled down, and a guy yells out, "Hey honey, wanna suck my—" I tune him out, pick up my pace and look straight ahead. He drives on. I walk another block under a dark sky and the same brown van is pulled over, engine running. "Hey honey ..." Everything in me wants to scream this guy off the planet. I bite my tongue, pretend to hear nothing. There's not one corner store or gas station, nothing, for five impossibly long blocks. Five blocks, not six, not four. In the absence of fear this detail would go unnoticed. Tonight it's a careful measure. I feel anything but tired now.

I decide to talk with him. After all, he's probably just a gentleman who is concerned for my health and welfare. Yeah that's it, he's offering me a ride home because I'm looking tired and it's not safe for a woman to be walking alone late at night. He's a Good Samaritan, a superhero type searching the dark city streets for women in distress. His only reward is knowing our safety is assured.

I swagger up to him. "Hi there, good-looking. Your name's Dick? Oh, I've always loved that name. It suits you. You're persistent, aren't you, Dick? I like a man who's assertive. A man who knows what he wants. You know, I don't want to waste your time with all this talk, so why don't we stop playing cat-and-mouse. We could head to the back of your van right now ... but I have a better idea. We could have a little fun at my place. I bet you know exactly what I want."

His mouth is hanging open and nothing but hot air is coming out. I step up into his van, apply a fresh coat of lipstick and slide right over until I'm nearly sitting in his lap. He follows my lead and feverishly grabs at my tits, as any other well-seasoned asshole in his position would do.

"Hey handsome, you know I want it bad, but it kinda turns me on to want something so bad it hurts. I'll be so horny by the time we get to my place I'll be on my knees just begging for a taste of your big cock." He grunts, shifts into first and off we go.

I climb the stairs with Dick following closely behind me. I feel his warm, uneven breath on the back of my kneecaps. He smells like stale beer nuts. I know he's hard. He thinks it's his lucky night. I purposely fumble with the keys, buying myself some thinking time. I unlock the door and turn around. We're face to face. Dick looks unsure of himself. In fact, he looks timid.

"Hey, why don't you make yourself comfortable? I'll pour us a drink and go freshen up." I lock the bathroom door behind me. I look in the mirror and see myself: a bitch-femme. My eyes are hard and dilated. Sound jars me. He is opening drawers, looking at magazines, touching objects, pawing through the life of a woman about whom he knows nothing. The hairs on my arms stand on end and my pulse quickens. I run my tongue slowly along my sharp teeth. I silently call on all of the bold bitch-femmes who have come before me, to be here, now.

I walk across my deep-red carpet, give Dick a coy sideways glance filled with a thousand empty promises. I pour one shot of Scotch, quietly sort through my cabinet and gather my props. Dick is looking out the window. I hand him the drink and run my index finger down his chest. He smirks and takes a swig. I smile back broadly and bring my right kneecap up sharply into his groin. Dick grabs his cock and crashes to his knees in a flurry of gags and spit. A beautiful sight; however, there's no time to wax poetic. Timing and precision is my verse now. While he's still down, I cuff him, kick him onto his belly and hogtie him.

"What the fuck are you doing, bitch—you cunt! I'm going to fuckin' kill you!"

"Excuse me? I don't think I heard you correctly. I'm a very direct person, Dick. I'm going to generously offer you my insights."

"Fuck off, bitch."

I squat on the floor and draw my favourite buck blade. "Don't mess with me. Don't say a fuckin' word!" My face is inches away from Dick's.

I stand brusquely, move hair away from my face. "Now, where was I? Oh right—I was offering you my insights when I was very rudely interrupted. Dick, it's very obvious to me that you have no one but yourself to credit for being in this position. That's right. You put yourself right here in the middle of my living room floor, on your belly, hog-tied. Don't you remember what your mamma said to you when you were a boy? You shouldn't talk to strangers. Especially women. You might just meet yourself some crazy bitch who'll chew you up and spit you out. Gotta be careful. Women—they're unpredictable, emotional, hysterical. Some of the things you and the boys talk about over beer are true. They'll turn on you. Don't give 'em an inch 'cause they'll take an arm. Bite it clean off and walk away smacking their lips.

"Dick, I could fuck you up. In case you haven't noticed, I have all the power right now. You have none because you're not intelligent enough to handle it. You are a moron, and tonight, Dick, you are a lucky moron. That's right. Lucky. I'm going to be easy on you because I don't want a mess in my apartment. You have my mamma to thank for that. She taught me to be neat, tidy and clear out the trash as soon as possible. So, this is what's going to happen. I'm going to let you go. Isn't that kind of me?"

I cut off his clothes. He's naked, and not nearly as threatening he was. I take in the sight of his white goose-pimpled skin against the red carpet. I feel some compassion for him, but not enough to be sincerely concerned with his state of well-being. I know the cuffs are cutting off his circulation. His hands and feet are numb. I sort through my trunk, making more noise than is necessary. I find exactly what I need. Duct tape.

"Oh yes, you are a lucky man. You should thank me ... I don't hear you."

"Thank you." His barely audible words sound more like a sneeze.

"Was that supposed to be a thank-you? One, I couldn't hear you under all of your shaking and two, you didn't thank me by name."

The sound of his laboured breath fills the room.

"You don't know my name, do you? I've been cordial enough to address you by your God-given name all fuckin' night, and you don't even know my name. You know, I should just kill you. I tell you, my mother is a saint, 'cause if it weren't for her you'd be dead right now. Remember this: my name is Anna. You are going to say: 'Thank you for sparing my cockroach life, Anna, and thanks to your mamma for raising you so well.' You are going to thank me right now."

Dick mutters into the carpet.

I find exactly what I need

"OK. That'll do. Now don't say another goddamn word and don't look back once I let you go."

I bite off a piece of duct tape and tape his keys between his shoulder blades. Drag him across the carpet until he's on the other side of my apartment door, unlock the ankle cuffs. Leave the wrist cuffs on and firmly lock the door.

I walk over to my window, light a cigarette and watch the smoke scatter as it hits the pane. The streetlight is buzzing more loudly than usual. Halfway through my cigarette, Dick stumbles out of my building. He's buck-naked, hunching over, trying to cover his cock.

He looks vulnerable.

Cold.

Scared.

duct

tape

ZOË

I was visiting my Aunt Lucia, my Uncle Matt and my cousin Aubyn Rose a few days after the Taste This performances in San Francisco. My cousin was at the kitchen table making cutouts for a miniature village she was creating. Her eyes were focused, soft but intent on the little piece of paper in one hand and the scissors in the other, changing the shape of things. Her pink little-girl lips neither frowned nor smiled as her fingers worked the paper. I used to do that as a child, build little worlds where everything was manageable in my small hands. I would decide the fate of all the characters and buildings, rooting out the bad guys, ensuring justice for all. Whole civilizations did whatever I wanted them to. They were blessed with good rainfall, the right amount of sun and good crops, or cursed by drought and earthquakes at the whim of my hands. But the world is not like that. Perhaps that's why miniature models are so important, and why I love them still.

I listened to my aunt talking to me from the kitchen as I placed spoons beside soup bowls. My aunt and uncle were concerned about Anna's story "superhero." They would prefer a more zen-approach to sexist assholes. They wanted to know if the story was based on truth or fantasy. Was it something a girl like Anna really would do? something she had even done? or was it a model of sorts, a dream about something she'd like to do to the next motherfucker who tries to intimidate her when she happens to be walking home alone after midnight? Either way it troubled them.

"I can only tell you how Anna has always answered that question," I said, placing bread and butter on the neatly checkered tablecloth. "Whenever anybody asks her if that story is true or not she just says, 'Makes you think, doesn't it? Makes you think.'"

Plastic Pearls

Lyndell

"We're warriors, wouldn't you say?" I asked, dressed in my best ripped jeans, painstakingly salvaged with forty-nine patches ranging in size, all hand sewn.

"What do you mean, warriors?" she asked.

"Look at you, Stick, look at us. Look at that woman over there. How much do you figure that damn coat she's wearing cost her? And the pearl necklace? Well, maybe it's rented."

Stick was catching my drift. "Get a load of those shoes, there's fucking rhinestones in them."

We were the only people in the opera house dressed for less than ten dollars (not including our boots), and damn we looked sharp. Who knew whether Yo-Yo Ma appreciated our style or not. I even polished my army boots and pressed my shirt, this was my tribute. Stick looks fine in anything she throws on. Tonight she looked particularly dazzling in her bright orange dress with fuzzy fruit deco, knee-high stockings and platform boots. Her plastic necklace accentuated her strong, high neck, blue eye-shadow accented deep-green eyes and sparkles glistened in her hair, pulled back into a tight braid. Never had so finely dressed a woman graced the opera house, I thought while looking at Stick.

A tuxedo- and gown-wearing couple sat down to our left. They looked at us sheepishly, looked away sharply when our eyes met theirs, smiles on our faces. They shifted and whispered discreetly.

"Good seats, aren't they?" Stick addressed the embarrassed duo.

"Yes, they are," came a deep-throated response from the man, his tone sharp. I'm sure he was thinking we were in the wrong place. We should have been washing the window of his Mercedes for a quarter.

"I love your dress," Stick exclaimed. I couldn't tell if she was toying or serious.

"Thank you," the woman replied. "It's a Giorgio Armani design." She spoke the words slowly, enunciating Giorgio as if she were solving the puzzle on "Wheel of Fortune" for $10,760.

"Are you fans of Yo-Yo?" I asked, leaning over Stick.

"Well of course. And yourself?" the woman asked smugly.

"Can't think of any place I'd rather be right now. I even ironed my shirt for the occasion." I smiled at her. She chuckled. Her date/husband/friend/escort cleared his throat.

I offered my hand. "My name is Devon."

She took it firmly to make it perfectly clear she was not intimidated by us. "Jane, my name is Jane and this is Evan." She released my hand and I exchanged grips with Evan as Stick introduced herself, her hand adorned with plastic rings from toy machines.

The rows behind us were slowly filling. Jane and Evan turned to each other, wishing they had not arrived early, wishing they weren't seated where they were, wishing we would stop talking to them. I looked at Stick and winked, she winked back. I leaned close, kissed her cheek lightly. "Thank you for bringing me tonight."

"Who else would I have brought, you fuck? No one else I know is brave enough to come to the opera house with me. You, however, find it stimulating, engaging, and you are so well behaved!" Stick joked. "Besides, my love, you need to be fed and tonight you are going to gorge on a five-course meal, served by none other than Yo-Yo Ma himself." I kissed her again, this time my hands on her face and my lips on hers. Bubble gum flavoured lipstick flooded my mouth. Our lips smacked as they parted. Evan and Jane turned toward the sound. Confusion spread over their faces as we moved from "Wheel of Fortune" to "Guess That Gender" game. We were winning. Evan is the boy and Jane the girl. Their eyes darted over my loose pirate shirt that covered tightly bound breasts, and rested for a daring moment on my crotch. It was there all right. The bulge that separates the sexes. I looked over my shoulder, pretended to be interested in what was behind me, allowing them the luxury of a longer look.

"What's the score?" I whispered to Stick.

"We're all tied up, except they probably think you're my kept boy."

"Well, you do have a penchant for young flesh," I teased. "You can't say it doesn't look a little suspicious and feel a little dangerous— you, the older woman sitting here with me, the pre-pubescent boy. I can see how our new friends might think you are giving me a cultural education."

It is a game that Stick and I play well. The boy and his keeper. If it weren't for the game, there are times I would lose my head. Sometimes a label is more comforting than none at all. Whether I am read as a gigolo, a pre-pubescent lad, a man-hating dyke or a lesbian, something is better than nothing. I don't always have the energy to explain myself. Sometimes I just need to go to the symphony.

So tonight I was a boy. My role was clear. I would pee into a cold toilet in the men's bathroom. Hold my cigarette between my thumb and index finger. Concentrate on keeping my voice on its leash.

Stick looked at me in that proud-to-know-you way. I sat tall. The house lights dimmed. "Enjoy the show, you two." Jane and Evan nodded and smiled in unison. I sank into the velvet seat, my hand resting on Stick's thigh. I closed my eyes. Dinner was served.

ZOË

ivan and i were sitting around at her place one afternoon with the sun sinking low over the park outside her window, nailing ideas to the gentle afternoon breeze and talkin' about folks who weren't around, about Lyndell and Anna and how much we miss 'em. well, it's no secret to folks who know us that Lyndell and i used to be lovers of the youngest most hopeful variety. living day-to-day and shooting for forever. we stopped being lovers about a year and a half before Taste This got together. by then Lyndell and Anna had fallen head over heels and were rolling happily through the honeymoon stage.

it's also no secret to folks who know us that ivan's always been a girl's boy and Anna's always been a boy's girl and Lyndell's always been a boy, period. i myself, though often thrown conveniently into the boy category by a community that should know better, have never really been completely comfortable with any label. if i reside anywhere it is in a place of shifting shapes and twilight, my favourite time of day. it is somewhere between the peace of solitude and the yearning for a lover's touch. it's a hard place to put your finger on and that's just fine with me.

as the afternoon turned to evening in ivan's living

room, I told her about me and
Lyndell back then, back when
it was all forevers that came
to an end.

I told Ivan, "I really was
in love with that boy."

And Ivan said, "Yeah, but
then he met a girl." Which is
not how it happened, but the
words still hurt and I told
her so.

"I didn't mean it like
that," Ivan said, "but you
know what I'm talking about."

I didn't, really, but I do
know a few things. I know that
nothing gets me hotter than a
beautiful boy/girl in a
finely tailored suit. I also
know that nothing makes me
feel quite as sexy as my 1940s
tuxedo complete with little
mother-of-pearl buttons and
cuff links, my hair slicked
back and shining. But then
again I look pretty good in
lipstick too.

141

142

Sly Boots
Anna

She looks like sly boots
　　strong-eyed and cocksure.
　She looks like borrowed diamonds
　　　in the rough and　　she is
　rough and raggedy,　　but never ragged
　　rough and tumble, but never falls
　rough around the edges, always sharp
　　rough housed, never caged
　　rough and ready　　always late.

　　She looks like lofty notions
　　　a high-handed harlot.
　　She looks like a slip stitch
　woven tight　　around her own groove.
　　She's a quick-tempered flame
　　　burning up the night
'cause there are no stars left in our urban sky
　　　'cause　　she can.

And to everyone who says the night's not safe
　　she says　　*what about closed doors*
　　　in bright buildings
　　what about all those locks?

143

She takes back the night with each step.
She's a brave bitch, a high-handed harlot
burning up   the night
lighting up   her own way.

She's a quick draw—
sits with her back to the wall
smart mouth at the ready
keys pressed between her fingers.
She learned a long time ago to never let 'em see your fear.
Smile only when you mean it
and look twice before you cross the road
'cause you never know what's coming.

She likes to think if she was in a bad way
if her hands were full and her tongue tied
her sistren and brethren would be at her back
holding her up
keeping her strong.

She likes her lovers soft on the inside and hard on the outside.
She likes tart fruit, strong coffee, colours that bleed
and stockings with runs.

She likes some things to be left unsaid—
stolen moments, borrowed time
and a fine glass of sherry.

She's the girl next door
who got away
who found the sky.
She's a one-eyed jack
a double-fisted queen
a wild card who
holds her hand close to her chest.

She looks like sly boots
strong-eyed and cocksure.

She looks like borrowed diamonds
in the rough and   she is
rough and raggedy,   but never ragged
rough and tumble, but never falls
rough around the edges, always sharp
rough and ready
always

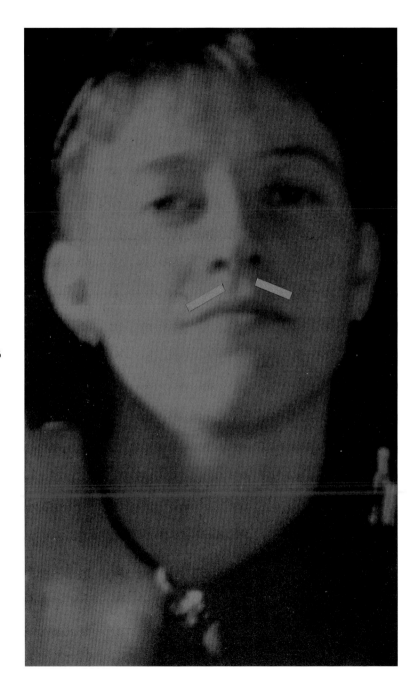

Manifestation
IVAN

I was working in the Yukon at the time, dry air, dirt under my nails, long days in the land where the summer sun seldom sleeps. It was six o'clock in the company truck, there was sand in my teeth and sweat left shiny trails through the dust on my face. We had planted and watered hundreds of trees that day, and I felt sunburnt.

My work partner, Kelly, was a sweet (until you crossed her) straight girl, due in two weeks to marry my old hockey buddy, Barry Fuller, also a landscaper. His parents lived in the industrial area of town, and my uncle used to date his older sister, Gale. Such is the small-town life and its folks.

I turned to say something to Kelly as she was driving.

"Oh my God, look at your face!" she interrupted me, red-faced. She was stuck between a laugh and a sort of half-gasp, eyes wide.

I tilted the rearview mirror toward the offending face and looked at my reflection. Sweat had run down my forehead and into the lines around my mouth. Perhaps I had passed a topsoiled hand over my upper lip, or maybe scratched an itchy nose with a dirty thumb, because there it was: a dirt mustache, worn perfectly into my top lip. Sweat lines and sprinkler spray had collected a perfect line of soil there, and I was transformed.

I looked just like a boy. To me, I looked like my long-lost brother. To my work partner, I looked like trouble.

"Here, here's a napkin. Wipe it off, you're creeping me out. You

wipe it off, you're creeping me out

look like my first boyfriend." She seemed a little nervous now, and would not meet my eyes.

"Is he a fag now, by any chance?" I enquired of her, my smirk pulling up one corner of my 'stache. I winked at her. "I'm gonna leave it, it's kinda sexy, don'tcha think? I bet the girls would love it, if there were any dykes in this godforsaken land."

She shook her head and shrugged, like she always did when I said anything queer, and kept driving.

I turned up the AM radio, sang a country tune about pick-up trucks, and looked in the rearview mirror. Couldn't help but look in the mirror, my eyes kept returning to my reflection, like a tongue to a loose tooth. Myself in a mustache. Something about it fit; it suited me, I thought.

That was the first one.

148

Silver Silicone
Sideshow

zoë

In the red-light district of Amsterdam, early in the fall and late in the evening, neon lights spill onto the canals, making the dingy water look like a radioactive technicolour dream. Jo and I cross the old stone bridge, ignoring offers for every mind-altering substance known to modern minds. We sidestep wide-eyed college boys ogling in front of windows framed in fluorescent pink, a silent brittle force field between them and the tired loveliness of bored-looking prostitutes. The women stare past them from plush armchairs, their eyes diving into the dirty canal. They are adding up figures in their heads to make rent, toying absently with lace hems and nibbling on nachos. People walk past like beads on an abacus.

We don't want drugs or paid physical contact, not now. Nothing must alter us from the course of our mission. First we need food; neither of us has eaten anything since breakfast. Then, on this our last night in Amsterdam, we are determined to see a live sex show.

We plunge noiselessly into the murmur, click and hum of the mottled cobblestone alleys on the other side of the bridge, in search of something cheap to fill our bellies. There are enough cheap food joints in the red-light district to feed a whole army of AmEx-packin' double-fisted doobie-smokin' adolescent coffeehouse philosophers on a munchy rampage. The trick is finding something within our one-meal-a-day budget that looks good when we're on a mission and not the least bit stoned.

We settle on a falafel joint and place our order: two falafels, extra everything, and two large waters. The guy takes our order and relays it to the guy at the grill. Then he turns and smiles, friendly enough, so we smile back. Then he allows a tentative curiosity to enter his eyes. He looks quizzically at Jo, and then at me, and then at Jo again. He says, "I want to ask you something but I'm not sure if I should."

"What did you want to ask?" queries Jo in that lazy, husky baritone that makes me not really care what she's saying as long as she says it in that voice. She's flirting with him in that nice-boy voice that isn't, that is only soft on the surface of its rolling notes, the tail end of her laughter still dancing in her eyes.

"Are you a boy or a girl?" The question comes stumbling forward like a drag queen in high heels.

"Sometimes, yes," says she. Then she steps back a pace as if to allow him a more thorough inspection and says, "Which do you think I am?" He looks now like he wishes for all the world that he'd stayed at the shallow end of the gender pool.

He shakes his head slightly, bites his bottom lip and says, "I don't know. I thought, but now ..." and with that the goddess of good timing, cleverly disguised as the grill guy, steps up to the counter with two falafels with extra everything. Jo, who never can resist, gives him a quick wink as we whisk our falafels off the battered arborite counter under his chin. We leave him with his cute predictable confusion and disappear to a table at the back.

We count our precious guilders while downing sandy falafel balls and retired tomatoes in tahini and hot sauce. If we skip every meal the next day except breakfast, which is provided by our hostel and served in a heavy cloud of hash smoke between the crack of dawn and 8:00 a.m., we have just enough money to go to the clean, well-lit club on the main drag that *Let's Go Europe* sanctions. Disliking this option, we decide that *Let's Go Europe* was addressed to weaker, less street-wise souls than us when it warns not to venture down the back alleys where the joints are seedier and you can bargain with the fast-talkers in fedoras and imitation Armani trying to get you inside for their pitiful commission.

We neatly polish off every last crumb of our humble purchase and wash it back with Styrofoam cups of water that tastes fresh from the canal. We top off the whole affair with a forgettable brand of cigarette that I couldn't and probably wouldn't buy at home, and we're off.

Back outside, the deep blue of late evening has matured into a fathomless black canvass. The streets are beginning to freak, boys in leather, studs and feather boas and women in fake-fur miniskirts and absolutely fabulous heels are splashing colour into the void. As we wander toward the back alleys with their salesmen, Jo talks about the last time she came here in less leather and more Gore-Tex.

She was just out of high school, doing Europe in the summer-time with a fresh-faced boyfriend at her side. That was before she'd said the word "dyke" out loud and meant herself. She was as straight looking then as was her thinking and she felt safe and sanctioned among confidently straight friends. But as they passed by one of these late-night sex-circus barkers, the man with the diamond-toothed smile contacted her with the whole circus in his eyes and said, "There's girls on girls too."

She recalls feeling a rather intense flush of discomfort for the briefest of moments. It was as though her head, heart and cunt all decided to jaywalk the same intersection from different corners, ending up butting heads in the middle of the street before scattering in different directions to avoid being flattened by oncoming traffic. The whole thing was rather quick and unnerving, and she decided to mistake her queasiness and the slight increase in her heart rate for a general outrage with the male-focused exploitiveness of it all. And now she wants to see a live sex show.

Liberation comes in strange packages, like her haggling at this very moment over the price of a peek with a man who less than a decade ago would have left her morally indignant. Tonight they are quibbling over whether throwing in the pre-show is worth an extra five guilders.

152

When we finally finish bargaining away money that we wouldn't be spending fighting for a glimpse of Rembrandt's "Night Watch," we're escorted through the underground door of a bar that looks for all the world like every other strip club I've ever been in, except it's smaller. The stage is a cute little semicircle up against the back wall, framed by bright yellow bulbs resembling a cheap pearl necklace. The place looks like a real cabaret. There are no curtains and no visible entrances or exits of any kind. For the moment the stage is profoundly empty. The same bad British and American pop music that seems to haunt me everywhere I go blares out over the souped-up sound system like a dull recurring nightmare, too familiar to be scary.

The bar is a strange affair, standing a few feet out from the wall on our right as we entered the theatre. It faces the stage and gives the illusion of camouflage. Sitting there means no one can see you from the lower chest down, while you have a full view of the rest of the theatre, except for the freaks beating their meat in the shadows. We instinctively choose to sit at the bar, swinging ourselves onto the high stools, legs apart, elbows on the counter.

We order a pint of the cheapest draft available straight off. The bartender is nice enough to be neither condescending nor coy when we order the most economical brew in the house. She's the kind of woman I like just by looking at her. Her thick, long, dark hair falls straight over her shoulders and down her back. She has a quick-draft hand and the skin and wrinkles of a remorseless partygoer who is probably younger than she looks. Her eyes are full of one-liners and her knowing smile is that of a woman who has done her time taking her clothes off in public. She serves us with a wink and a grin. We smile and nod back.

Jo and I each light a smoke and survey the crowd, waiting, inhaling deeply, smelling the usual strip-club smells: stale smoke, spilled beer and sweat. We decide to spring for another beer. By the time the bartender places two glasses in front of us, the back door swings open to reveal the most tight-bodied celluloid-looking creature in a top hat that I've ever seen. She has a sweet smile, the kind you could taste from a distance, and an apple pie face that makes you want to run out and buy vanilla ice cream. Her legs have a will of their own. When she high-kicks, her knee meets her nose and her legs seem to cover roughly the same distance I had while travelling Europe by boat, train and bus. In one hand she carries a dildo modelled after an over-sized silver bullet. She places it at the centre front of the stage, leaving it there while she does a hard-rock flash dance, strategic stray curls sweeping her shoulder blades as she swings her hips from side to side.

The dildo looks like a disembodied icon placed on guard duty, stoic and sorely upstaged all on its own like that, what with her slow twirling limbs and impossibly tight muscles doing a well-practiced ripple only metres away. Halfway through her second song—and naked except for a black bowler hat and high black boots laced up to just below her knees—she tilts the rim of her hat forward, its shadow cutting sharp lines on her high cheekbones. She casts a slow critical look about the room. The closer her eyes come to where we are sitting, the tighter my clothing feels, the warmer the room seems, until my entire body threatens to combust when her eyes come neatly to rest on Jo and me.

There we are, caught like rabbits in the headlights of an on-coming convertible. I had been about to sip my beer but this turn of events seems to require my full attention. Her eyes don't budge or falter and it's clear that she has made her choice, but I'm not sure which of us she's chosen. She puts her left palm forward and crooks her index finger back toward her palm, just once, that's all. I feel Jo blush before I actually see it on her face. She has been summoned. I breathe a sigh of relief and then, making no effort to hide the voyeuristic grin on my face, I lean toward her, my voice low enough for her alone, and say, "Go on, baby, make my night."

At first she shakes her head No in a gentlemanly decline. Her caller, however, is not so easily dissuaded. She cocks her head to one side and smiles a smile too lovely to be coy. Suddenly Jo rises from her stool like a snake summoned by flutes. She makes her way past small tables, up over the row of cheap pearl lights and past the earnest-looking dildo until she is standing directly in front of the hand that summoned her.

Jo looks vulnerable and timid up there, as though she were the one standing there naked. Her hostess looks confident, her smile reassuring and flirtatious, as though she were fully clothed before this blushing boy. I wonder from which well her confidence springs. I wonder if she has any idea of the shapes that shift under the sagging denim disguise worn by the freckle-faced figure before her.

There isn't long to wonder. In the slow sultry wink of an eye she dances Jo up to the centre of that little stage with her back to the wall. Hips grinding to the music, she eases the plaid sack of a shirt free from the half-hearted grasp of a low-strung belt. Slowly and teasingly she lifts it up over Jo's belly, and then I get my answer.

There is the briefest split-second hesitation when she sees the tight Lycra sports bra that conceals Jo's small, round breasts. It was one of those moments that seem like hours. I think I feel Jo and the stripper and the whole room hold their breath. Maybe it was just me.

Instantly, instinctively my queer eyes scan the room for hostile reactions, ready to stand and fight or fend off. More likely is the scenario now playing itself out in my head: me plucking Jo off the stage with one hand and throwing her jacket over her with the other, bolting for the door and the nearest dark alley. To my relief my scan provides no cause for alarm. The audience's reaction ranges from bored to fascinated to still oblivious. I allow myself to breathe again and the moment passes.

When I turn back to the stage, Jo's shirt has been slipped easily over her broad shoulders and deposited neatly on the floor at her feet. Her cheeks are still cherry red and a cocky grin is beginning to frolic around her lips. She has just gender-fucked a professional and it is just now dawning on her that she will probably live to tell about it.

She doesn't have long to be pleased with herself, though. This woman has a standard routine to execute in a limited number of verses. Gender-fuck or no, she has wasted valuable seconds hesitating over Jo's sports bra and she isn't about to waste any more time. More quickly than a tourist can get his wallet lifted at a European train station, she has Jo's belt out of its loops and her hands bound behind her back with more than an inch of leather left to spare. With a firm and gentle hand she leads Jo away from the back wall and down onto her knees in preparation for the silver bullet dildo's moment of glory.

She takes it from where it so patiently waited at the foot of the stage and deposits its base neatly in the firm grip of Jo's teeth. The stripper slides her hips in close, not more than a foot away from that silicone sentinel. Jo's grin is back full force now. Even with her mouth full I can see it splitting open. This is a game she knows how to play and she is going to win it. She would faint from exhaustion before admitting defeat. Her effort is valiant to say the least, hands straining against tightly bound leather. She reaches skyward for leverage as she leans and lunges forward. Every time she comes within an inch of that practiced, artful pussy, its owner wiggles her hips over black boots and shimmies just out of reach. You'd think she'd done this before.

156

The crowd begins to stomp and holler as Jo gives it her all, rearing back and pitching forward with reckless abandon, sweat breaking on her brow. Just as it becomes clear that she will never touch that sacred fruit, just as her efforts begin to reach their highest pitch, the whole experience bordering on painful, the stripper stops. Standing just out of reach, she stills Jo with one gentle palm and strokes her bowing shoulders and bent neck. She takes the dildo out of Jo's mouth and smiles into her eyes. Gathering up her clothes, she ruffles Jo's short-cropped hair and disappears out the back door of the theatre. There is something very matter-of-fact about her nakedness as she leaves the stage, as though she had gotten up in the middle of the night to go to the bathroom.

A couple of dutiful college boys in the front row help Jo's hands out of their leather grip and are sweet enough or stoned enough or both to pat her on the back like a brother who has just returned from war. She makes her way exhausted and shining back to the stools we had thought would hide us so well. I tell her the next beer is on me even if I have to forego meals for a week. We raise a toast to cheap beer and the unexpected, as the grand finale begins.

The grand finale amounts to a tired-looking couple wearing matching black silk briefs and carrying out a ragged imitation-bearskin rug. They fuck in six different profoundly mechanical positions, all to the tune of Madonna's "Vogue": "Strike a pose, there's nothing to it." They never miss a beat or come that I can see. The woman is a brassy blond who is undoubtedly going over a list of things to do tomorrow in her head. She keeps her showbiz smile neatly on her face from beginning to end. The man has red hair and a handlebar mustache that makes him look like an underfed lion-tamer. He pumps away earnestly, his brow lined with strain and concentration until the song ends and his job is done. They take their bows and leave the stage, back into street clothes and home to a well-earned rest. Another night, another fuck.

... And Jo and I? Well, we put our arms around each other and let our feet wind a lazy path back the way we came. Past the freaks and the college boys and the tired beauties framed in pink neon. Back to our dingy eight-by-five-foot room on the wrong side of the canal. Laughing as we go, we tease each other and say, "Well, you don't always get what you came for."

another

fuck

LYNDE

I just forget sometimes, you know. It's not that I think I'm invincible, I just refuse to walk around with my back to the wall and my eyes always searching for a fist or bottle or comment being hurled my way. This is not to say that I possess a seventh sense for trouble or that I'm not grateful for a watchful eye beside me and a protective hand held tightly in my own. I just forget that being different is still wrong. especially if you're stopping for gas in a small American town in oregon.

My hair is blue and spiked in twenty carefully crafted points. Ripped army shorts, hairy legs, tattoos, facial piercing and a T-shirt with bold letters all declare that I am a FAG. My voice is too high-pitched to be male and my breasts are outlined by the shirt against my body. I was pumping gas into our car and chatting with Ivan, who was busy washing the windows and checking the oil level.

on the other side of the gas bar stood a jacked-up 4 x 4, looking like it was right out of <u>A TIME TO KILL</u>. A National Rifle Association sticker was stuck on the back window just underneath, you guessed it, the gun rack. shiny chrome roll bars and tires to fit a tractor turned this average 4 x 4 into a machine. I replaced the gas cap and went in to pay, taking my time, looking for treats.

I felt the eyes before I saw them. They belonged to a bearded giant of a man who was stopped dead in his tracks, looking at me. our eyes locked and in an instant I realized that no one around would tell the truth about how I'd lost my life in the convenience store of a red-neck town. why would they bother telling the truth? what would it be? That my blue hair was offensive?

"your honour, his T-shirt and voice didn't match. Nothin' about him matched. people like him give hard-work-ing Americans a bad name." The sign by the cash register states "alcohol, cigarettes and firearms sold here." oh man I was screwed. I had hoped I would always be intuitive enough to avoid situations like this. I knew I should scramble for the door before my head was smashed in, but I couldn't move. I was frozen, standing over my already-dead body watching the local authorities manoeuvre.

My bloody corpse as the centrepiece, the cops were taking statements about how I had come at the giant with a knife. yeah, that's it, a knife. other customers would describe how he wrestled it away from me and protected himself. The cops would nod in an empathetic manner, pat the giant on his back and tell him how he'd done the right thing. No one would remember what happened to the knife I supposedly wielded and the cops wouldn't bother collecting it for evidence.

The door to the store swung open and Ivan stood in its frame, small in the shadow of the man between us. The funeral parlour music in my head shut itself off; now all I could hear was the beating of my heart. Ivan had come for me, sensing trouble, smelling blood about to be spilled. My blood, our blood, a small town's hate. slowly I felt around in my pocket for a twenty-dollar bill. clenching it tightly in my fist, I eased my hand from my pocket.

The man's eyes were still on me, his breath heavy, his fists clenched at his side. we had not spoken a word to each other, but I wasn't about to start talking. Ivan stood motionless in the door frame, propping the door open with his boot. only the clock behind the counter made any noise. Tick, tock, tick, tock, tick .... suddenly Ivan let out a yell that sounded like a pig being slaughtered. The giant wheeled around and in that instant I threw the twenty on the counter and bolted past him out the door. Ivan and I sprinted toward the car, jumped in, and Anna squealed away, doors slamming as we sped off. The Taco Bell advertisement ran through my head, "Make a run for the border."

Sweet Boy
Anna, Ivan & Lyndell

Anna

Sweet Boy. You came to me with your callused hands stuffed into your pockets and your eyes unable to hold my gaze. You came to me knowing next to nothing about girls. Of course, this girl is not the same as the next; nonetheless, you knew next to nothing. So I was patient and gentle with you.

Lyndell

And enraptured I was when she looked at me and called me her sweet boy. "My sweet boy," she said. Which word was it that tugged at me most strongly? Each held its own meanings, memories, fantasies, lies and truths.

Ivan

How to describe to the uninitiated what sort of peace it is that steals over the soul of the servant in me when with tips of soft fingers you lift my face from your lap so I might see your lips move to call me a sweet boy? What solace it seems when you lift my real name from inside me like this and say it aloud, breathe life into this secret spirit of mine. *Sweet Boy* you slip inside my skin and make me an angel when you say it, *sweet boy, you are such a sweet boy.* It brings me wings just to think of it, this is the truth as I know it to be.

Tell me, five and ten years ago, what would you have called your ten-year-old tomboy when she was on her best behaviour? If you were to call her a "good girl," she might not know it was she who had pleased you, for she might not know she was a girl at all. Perhaps she sees no reflection of herself when she watches the other girls; she knows that she is different somehow, she can sense this but does not have any word that describes herself. And, as she bears no overt traits belonging to either gender, or shows signs of both, it is often demanded of her by strangers that she define herself for them in this way: "You a boy or a girl?" She has been taught to fear God, and adults, and so she always responds, though she hates the question. She is told there are only two possible answers, yet neither of these rings completely true to her ear, as she has explored both options and both leave the taste of a lie in her mouth. If there are no words to describe what she is, then maybe she does not exist at all, and is it a sin to be a creature that God had no name for?

Anna

I took you by the hand to my bed after idle conversation. I let your sticky fingers gently touch my face and collarbones and nervously by-pass my breasts. I noticed your laboured breathing and swelled underneath it.

Lyndell

My. It suggests ownership and possession, and depending on the tone of the voice, perhaps pride. She sounded full of pride when she spoke it, calling me hers and knowing that I was. Willingly, longingly and completely. There was power in this word *my*. I knew it and she knew it. It meant I would fetch her tea, help her put her jacket on, lick her boots and kiss her fingertips when permitted. *My* ... interpreted as hers. And I was.

Ivan

She knew she was not a boy; she had been made painfully aware of this already. Of this there could be no doubt, she had been told too

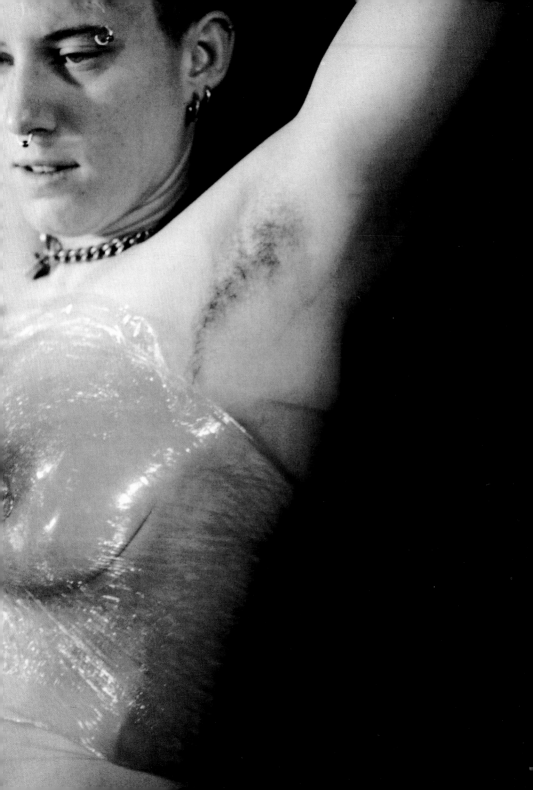

many times. Yet she felt no affinity to the female sex either. To her real girls were an even stranger species than boys, their games made no sense, held no reason for her at all.

So you see, it is of no use to call a tomboy a "good girl." This means nothing to her, and she might even take offence at your term, depending on the sort of a tomboy she is. How many gracious tomboy tasks have gone unthanked for this reason?

Anna You offered me your innocence, sweet boy. You told me that you felt like a teenager who had been sent by his father to a high-priced mistress. You even spoke to a femme friend of yours to learn about us girls. I asked you what you learned and you shyly said, "You're wearing garter underneath your kilt." You were right, on that particular night, and I told you so. You looked proud of yourself, and being the smart boy that you are, you quickly added, "I've never actually removed garter." I graciously assisted you by demonstrating the unfastening. You seemed surprised by the simplicity and ease of the ritual.

164

Ivan She called herself a femme. It was a matter left up to her to decide, for her to let me know that she was one of my kind. I had made it safe for her because of how I looked. This is the dilemma of the gentle-butch: how am I supposed to make the first move, which she is expecting, when maybe she's straight, maybe she'll call in her boys on me and I could get hurt and I hate pain.

Lyndell Sweet. The word rolled off her tongue and lodged itself in my heart, cunt and ass. It slit my flesh and slid its five letters into my veins, stirring my blood. It wrapped itself tightly inside my throat making breath stagnant ... until the word *boy* touched my ears so lightly that it left no trace of evidence that it had even been there at all. But I had heard it. She called me a *boy*. My attention was hers entirely as the

word boy always causes my ears to perk and my eyes to come into steady focus. *Boy,* it made me squirm.

I have always been this, that is the difference between her and me, you see. I do not mean to say that all butches were once tomboys or that all tomboys grow up to be queers or all dykes who wear dresses were once proper little ladies, blah, blah, blah. That is not what I am saying.

Anyway, she was in a red velvet dress that night, femme fatale. The birthday girl got what she wanted—the young gentleman in the

166

third row, second one in please, have her come to my dressing room during intermission. Her message boy came to find me outside smoking, how could I refuse, she had called me a gentleman, and she was, after all, quite the lady.

Anna

Your eyes were big and round with curiosity. You looked like a child playing hide-and-seek. You weren't sure if you were it or if I was it. You weren't sure of the rules. Sweet boy, had you asked me what I know about boys I probably would have said, "Enough to make you uncomfortable," or I may have said, "More than you care to know." Or I may have pushed you onto your back without saying a word and showed you, as I did in fact do, later on. None of these answers is straight-up, is it? None of these answers is really an answer at all. Isn't that just like a girl? An innocent boy asks a fair question and gets caught in a sticky web he couldn't see.

Lyndell

Boy. It breathed life into my lungs. I was to her what I was not to others looking in and on. I was a boy to her. A sweet boy.

Ivan

Sweet boy you call me *what a good sweet boy you are* and it rings so true, so straight to my centre, how to describe the comfort of hearing you call me this name? I was never truly a good girl, you see, and it was vaguely not OK to be so good at boy things but not good enough to be a boy. Tomboys try so hard to be everything but they can never really work it either way, so now your voice seems such sweet magic, honey down my spine. You want what I really am, a sweet boy. The first time you took me like a boy it seemed so easy. You fucked me into a stupor—now I know what fucked your brains out means. "You are such a good boy," you said. "Sweet boy, turn over on your belly, Ivan, I would never hurt you." But you lied, and you did, and I was glad of it too. A boy needs some discipline if he is to one day make a good father, become a provider. You are for my own good, of this I am sure. I only pray I can taste as sweet to you as these words of yours sound to me.

Anna

Sweet Boy. You came to me with your callused hands stuffed into your pockets and your eyes unable to hold my gaze. You came to me knowing next to nothing about girls. Of course, this girl is not the same as the next; nonetheless, you knew next to nothing. So, I was patient and gentle with you.

Lyndell

And enraptured I was when she looked at me and called me her sweet boy. "My sweet boy," she said.

Luan

How to describe to the uninitiated what sort of peace it is that steals over the soul of the servant in me when with tips of soft fingers you lift my face from your lap so I might see your lips move to call me a sweet boy? What solace it seems when you lift my real name from inside me like this and say it aloud, breathe life into this secret spirit of mine. *Sweet Boy* you slip inside my skin and make me an angel when you say it, *sweet boy, you are such a sweet boy.* It brings me wings just to think of it, this is the truth as I know it to be.

Border Crossing: No Underwear
anna

We spent our last night and day in Seattle with new-found friends;
eating, talking, laughing, flirting, enjoying each other's company. I
leave their home feeling sexy and sated—the taste of delicious food
dancing on my tongue. We pile into our car and I jump into the driver's seat, bound for the border.

As we approach the Customs booth, I review my pat replies out
loud: "We were in Seattle for two nights and two days. We bought cigarettes. Receipts are in the glove box. Citizenship: Canadian. We were
visiting friends. Remember, nothing about performing or writing …
it's taxable," I reiterate to my friends. Zoë and Ivan nod. Lyndell turns
down the stereo. I check myself in the rearview mirror. I look fairly
calm despite my last border experience; I had been body searched.

I answer all of the guard's questions efficiently. He waves us to
the side without offering an explanation. "Fuck!" we mutter in har-
mony. I pull off to the left. Vehicles carrying happy passengers fly
past. Two large uniformed men instruct us to step away from our car.
We comply.

The guards waste no time. Our possessions are removed and
scattered on the concrete. Tension, sharp and pointed, rises like a wall
between us. We simultaneously draw cigarettes from our respective
packs. Ivan offers each one of us a light. Lights his own last.

The smaller man of the two opens Lyndell's case, shakes her
violin as though it were a baby rattler. Lyndell walks up to the guards. I

can't hear her, but I know she is asking them to be careful. The exchange is brief. Lyndell rejoins us. "Look at what they're doing to my violin! If anything happens, I'll freak." She kicks at stones, her voice rises. "I can't replace her. Who the fuck do they think they are?" The guard tears the velvet lining away from the case. Lyndell's sheet music is scattered, along with a photograph of her newly found biological mother. "Fuck this!" Lyndell begins to make her way toward them again.

All three of us jump in front of her. "Lyndell, it's not right that we got pulled over, and that we always get pulled over. It's not right that they can do whatever the fuck they want. But that's the way it is. I personally would like to leave with some dignity—"

Lyndell interrupts me: "Look at what they're doing!"

"Lyndell, I don't have any underwear on under my goddamn kilt because I was feeling so good back at Dragon and Billy's place that I temporarily took leave of my senses. Look—the fuckers are going to fuck with us until they're done. Hopefully we'll be able to go home sooner than later. Calm down! They're gonna mess with us even longer if they see our fear. Don't give it to them."

Zoë jumps in, "I'm sorry, Lyndell."

Ivan puts his arm around Lyndell's shoulder, "Come on brother, let's go for a walk." Just as they are sauntering away, the guards' voices chime in hearty laughter. They're reading from Ivan's leather-bound journal. I'm enraged. That journal is Ivan's Bible. He writes *everything* in there. Ivan who always has words, has no words. Runs fingers through his fine hair, shakes his head. Lyndell puts her arm around Ivan.

My mother's ominous childhood warning about clean underwear runs through my head. Zoë and I stand in silence. I don't know what's going through her head, nor do I ask. When we look up, the bigger guard is holding Lyndell's red dildo, affectionately know as Rex, between index finger and thumb. A blush, an unmistakable pink blush, rises to their white faces. Lyndell and Ivan rejoin us, with smirks on their faces.

"He's touching my dick," Lyndell muses. "Funny, I don't feel a thing."

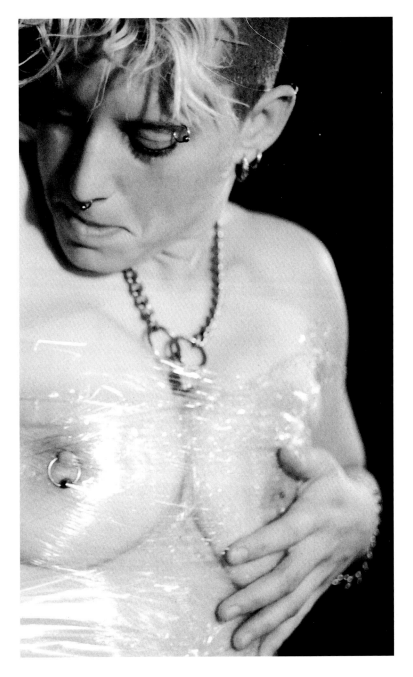

She Told Me

Ivan

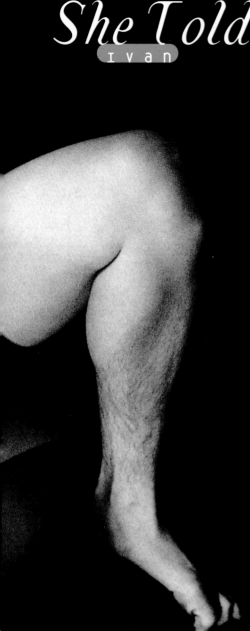

She told me her name was Lipstick. This only after I had offered up mine, and then still had to ask for hers.

I had been watching mostly fags dancing to mostly fag dance music when my eyes stopped and stuck on the sight of her neck. Skin music it was, the way her shoulders turned slender and arched up to meet her close-shorn head, unmistakably female. She turned around and trapped my gaze in hers. Caught staring. Good one.

She did not smile coyly and then ignore me, as many would. She did not just ignore me, either. She did not even smile. She unfolded one long arm in my direction, first finger extended, turned her wrist and cocked one eyebrow, and curled her finger twice, from me to her, *Come here.*

It was not a request. It was not an order. I thought about it later, and decided what it was: a statement. A statement of fact. *If I curl my first finger just like this, the tomboy in the tight black shirt will come.*

Dance with her.

Six or seven songs in a row, her hands finding one of my hips and the small of my back, effortlessly, we never missed a beat. I'm not sure now who was leading, two bodies, one motion, until sweat wet our hair and stuck our shirts to our backs. I never even stepped on her feet, not once. She must have been leading, come to think of it.

Finally, out of breath and with ice water in my hand, I told her my name, and asked hers.

I don't know how many of you have ever travelled on a lake that is fed by glacier water, but that's what colour her eyes were. Light bright green, but with grey underneath, that combination of mountain pure and all that the mountain is made of, sand, silt and minerals. Glacier water looks like it should be clear but is not; it's the kind of cold that burns if you put your hand in it. The kind of cold that pulls the piss and the breath from your body and leaves you with blue lips. That was the colour of her eyes, and she told me her name was Lipstick.

Red mouth, black hair, green eyes.

Green eyes that passed over, up and down the outside of me like I was a melon at the Save-on-Foods: *is this a keeper, or not, will it be too soft around the middle in a couple of days to eat?* That was what her eyes said. Which is not to say it was a bad feeling, or, that I did not enjoy it.

"Lipstick your real name?" For reasons unexplainable still, I asked her one of those stupid questions I hate answering myself.

An almost pointed tongue ejected the straw in her cocktail from her mouth, and she looked at me with something approaching scorn, or was it boredom, biting the ends of her words:

"And I'm sure your fucking parents called you Ivan when you were a little girl."

We both laughed at this, and didn't talk much more. She took my phone number home that night, and I didn't hear from her for about two weeks.

Her voice sounded a bit deeper on the phone. "I'm having a couple of friends over for a late lunch this Sunday, they'll be here about two. I'd like for you to be here, about twelve, twelve-thirty, is that OK for you?"

She lived on the second floor of a classic character house, just slightly west of where I usually travel to visit friends. That Sunday was overcast and cool, and the shuttered windows of her suite over-looked the front yard, making her house look like one big sleepy face as I approached.

The doorbell rang hollow in the hall, like old house hardwood floor doorbells do, and then I heard her footsteps. When she filled the door frame, she spoke first. This was to become a bit of a pat-tern, her doing most of the talking.

"Hey, Ivan, come on in, don't worry about your boots, the woman downstairs, the landlady, sweet old thing, she's a little hard of hearing, it works perfect, really. Here, I'll show you where to put your coat."

I followed her up the stairs and into her apartment, down the hall and into her kitchen, still silent.

"Everything's in here, everything you'll need. We're having poached eggs and sautéed vegetables, in vol-au-vent pastry. Don't worry, they're frozen, you just pop them in the oven, you'll be fine. And hollandaise sauce. The orange juice is in the fridge, and please, don't make the coffee until the guests arrive. I'm going to lie down for a bit, my head aches a little."

I stood there in the door of her kitchen, my coat half on, half off. I guess the shock must have registered in my face. Her eyes laughed as she spoke through her smirk: "I said I was having a late lunch, I did not say I was going to cook. I asked around a bit about you, someone told me you could make yourself useful around the house, if you put your mind to it. Better start separating your yolks, big boy, you were ten minutes late. I'll be in my room if you absolutely can't find something."

It wasn't until later, alone in her kitchen, chopping garlic, that I realized that I still hadn't said anything.

That was our first date.

The next time I saw her was unexpected, a one-too-many-nights-out-with-the boys kind of evening. I was on my way to the last bathroom stall when a long-fingered hand found my necktie and pulled me into the middle booth. She shut the door behind me with her boot and pulled my face up to hers. Her other hand had the short hairs at the back of my neck, lips just an inch from mine. "Well look, if it isn't the hired help. You look cute in a suit."

I have always appreciated a woman who knows what she wants in bed. I especially appreciate a woman who knows what she wants in a public bathroom stall.

The floor was cold and unforgiving but, caught up in the moment as I was, it didn't hurt my knees at all. I remember her nails on my shoulder blades and both my hands slipping under and up to slide her skirt over her ass to her hips, and it was over before my neck got sore.

She pulled my face up close to rest on her warm belly, and ran her fingers through my hair, her one leg still over my shoulder. Wet whispers passed between us, until someone pounded on the door.

"Come on you two, enough already, some of us actually have to pee, and there's a line-up out here. Hey ... is that you, Ivan?"

It's the one unfortunate thing about these trendy Caterpillar boots of mine. The bright caterpillar-yellow bottoms are all too easily identifiable, should one ever be caught soles up.

It's true, you know. Homosexuals do have sex in public bathrooms. We can't help ourselves. It's a DNA thing.

She eventually fucked me, later that night at her place. I needn't go into the details here, in mixed company, but I'll give you a hint: she left me with a bite mark on the *back* of my neck.

She was most definitely my kind of girl.

So there we were. Me and my kind of girl, a couple of days later in that mostly veggie sandwich place on the Drive, she poised and I slouched on the tall stools by the front window counter. She was feeding me little bits of salad and I was reading her the paper.

I made some smart-ass remark that escapes me now, and she knuckle-punched me right in that insta-hurt part of my upper arm.

"Hey, owww ... fuck ... you punch like a girl."

I should have regretted these words as soon as they left my fool mouth, but too much sex has been known to make me stupid.

"Sit up straight and watch your fucking mouth, or I'll slap that cocky smile right off of it for you." She spoke through clenched teeth, hardly moving her painted lips.

The hippies slurped tomato basil soup beside us, not one sensing the peril the smart-mouth on the stool was placing herself in.

"You wouldn't hit me in front of all these vegans ..." The cocky smile was halfway from my brain to my face when it was intercepted. By the palm of her hand. I felt the ground give under my ass, and all eyes were on me as I hit the floor tiles. Next I was aware of my now-empty stool rocking back on two legs a couple of times before deciding not to fall on top of me.

Not a soup spoon moved for a moment. *Hmm ... vegetarians leave wads of gum under countertops too.* I remember this ridiculous thought passing through my rattled brain just before her voice brought me back to my wits.

"Just for that, I'm going to let you buy lunch." She whirled on one wide heel and walked out.

I picked myself up and avoided all eyes as I settled the bill, my ears burning.

I should stop right here and make it quite clear that I am not generally the kind of person who likes to be dragged about, slapped around, or sexually, financially or domestically exploited. Not unless it is done with a certain amount of flair.

Over time, four, five months maybe, we came to know certain parts of each other very well. Intimate strangers, we were. I knew the smell of her, even in my sleep, but I did not know where she worked, or even what she did for work. I knew the insides of her, her folds and her corners. I knew what she tasted like between her toes, I knew how her breath changed just before she fell asleep, but I did not know her last name, or what her father did for a living, or if her mother was still alive. She never offered me up any of these details, and so I never asked. Most of the time, this didn't bother me.

One time, though, in her bed, in that deep-blue time where night isn't just night anymore, but part first light, she shook me awake.

"You were screaming, Ivan. You screamed. It was only a bad dream. It's just you and me here. Just me, and you."

She pulled my head down to her chest, her body circling mine. She gripped her right nipple between two fingers, parted my lips and put her nipple into my mouth. Her thumb traced the shape of my face and then brought its wetness to her lips. Her tongue tasted my tears. And my tongue tasted her ... *breast milk?* I have only tasted breast milk one other time in my adult life, but there could be no mistake, its taste stains your mouth sweet, and lives still in the back of your throat long after you swallow.

I don't remember any words after that. Sleep was easy, and I dreamt empty.

A few hours later, I awoke before she did. I wanted to wake her up and talk, but I didn't. I wanted to tell her about nightmares and what I wanted to be when I grow up, but I didn't. I wanted to ask her about breast milk, about her brothers, about where she was born. I wanted to ask her about the long thin scar that runs up the centre of her belly, but I didn't.

Instead, I slipped from beneath the covers and padded quietly to the kitchen, to put the coffee on. I dressed silently, sitting on the bed beside the still sleeping sheet-covered shape of her. She opened her eyes just as I was about to close the bedroom door.

"I like it that you know when to leave," she said, smiling slowly at me. Her voice didn't sound like she had just woken up.

The door shut behind me with a soft click.

It wasn't until about ten days had passed without hearing from her that I began to wonder what was up.

180

I called. Her phone rang for no reason, as apparently there was no one there to pick it up.

Two weeks gone, wonder turned to worry, so I was forced to break one of the rules. That being, don't just drop in on the mysterious sex stranger or you run the risk of revealing just the right dose of reality at precisely the wrong moment, which can be fatal to a previously flawless fantasy. I know this.

Still, I walked over to her house, without an invitation, and knocked. She did not come to the door. Her landlady was in the front yard, planting tulip bulbs with a small red spade.

"Have you seen the girl who lives on the second floor?" I spoke slowly and loudly.

She narrowed her landlady eyes at me. She was wearing flowered garden gloves, and she used one dirty hand to pull the front of her shapeless grey cardigan over her stomach.

"She went home."

Home? My eyebrows arched in a question mark.

"Yes. Yes. Home," she returned sharply, showing the lines in her forehead. "She went home to Winnipeg, to be with her family. I was so sorry to see her go. Such a nice girl." She paused, and her eyes flashed on me (not a nice girl, sorry to see me go). "She never make a problem for me, that one. She was a good girl, that Linda."

She knelt again to her flower bed. This conversation was officially over. My breath steamed in front of me as I walked up her street to catch the bus. The wind picked up a bit, and I pushed my hands into my pockets.

Winnipeg? I thought to myself, shaking my head. She told me she was from San Francisco.

Linda? She told me her name was Lipstick.

181

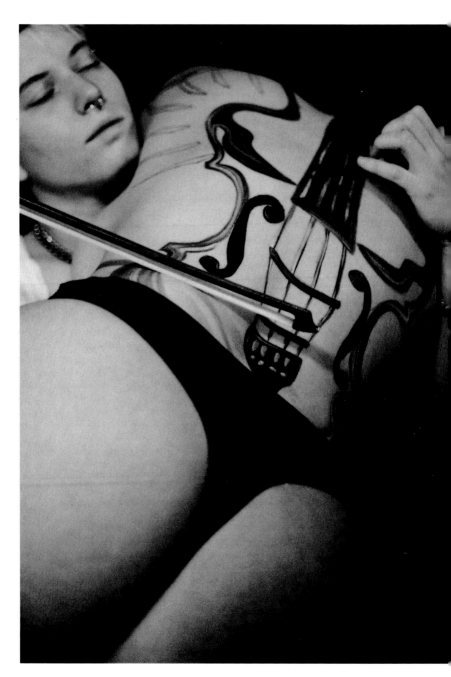

182

Mermaid

I had been waiting a long time. Cold from my naked skin colliding with the damp floor of the basement suite. The floor was blue. A shade that makes you think of the Mediterranean Sea. Blue that you see right through, but what you see on the other side is more blue, forever blue, melting into itself. I know, because I was staring at it for so long. Maybe I was there for half an hour, maybe all afternoon, time evades me. It was long enough that the floor melted into ocean, back to floor, into sea and then floor again.

Tipping my head back, I was engulfed by yellow. The light fixture was the sun, kissing my cold, bare body, blazing heat as I lay on the sea floor waiting.

I knew she would come to me, but I did not know when. She would come in her time and I would wait on that time, hoping. I could hear her. The clink of thin metal coat hangers, the familiar sound of her make-up case opening. Just a zipper, but I knew that sound by how quickly it came and disappeared again. The opening of the make-up case meant lipstick. What colour? Magenta? Twig? The sound of plastic through fabric touching wood. Silence. She was looking at herself in the mirror. One hand arranged fire-like hair. Red, orange, blue and white flames licked forth from her head. The other hand pulled a tightly wound curl to hang over seductive bitch eyes. She turned to the right to examine her ass, to the left to eye the

curve of her hip. Both hands under her breasts, arranging them perfectly on the shelf of a push-up bra.

My eyes open and I am looking at my white skin, brown from
the season, under a black harness. Legs tight, muscles showing. Tense.
A current moves me in and out of warmth. The throw rug looks like
a bottom-fish resting, eyes open, partially buried in sand. Silence sur-
rounds me as I sit, still on the sea floor and wait for her to enter its
depths, enter me.

I smell her, look up and see the mermaid hovering above me.
Hint of a smile on her smug face. Black glossy scales moving over me.
Gentle, exploring, dangerous. No eye contact, not yet. Self-con-
scious, naked in humanness, afraid, alive. Electricity flows in the current, white bolts jolting my flesh. She moves behind me, her even
breath keeps me still. Hands on my neck. I breathe in, dissect oxygen, send back water. Hands tighten, pull me to my feet. A hard kick,
my legs collapse, I'm face down, butt up against the rocking chair. I
want to breathe, can't. A touch, a breath. Her touch leaves, I gag on
sea water. She's playing with me. Proving a point. My life is in her
touch. She circles around, our faces inches apart. I can see her teeth.
Pointed, sharp. Not afraid to use them, cut her prey apart. Backing
away she curls a finger, beckoning. Offering breath, life, in exchange
for submission. Lungs burn. I comply.

My face within tongue's reach of glistening leather boots. Fist in
my hair, I breathe cool water turned air. She pulls me to my knees,
draws my mouth to her cock. I split my lips with my tongue to take
her in. Lips on the head of her cock. I reel backward with the force
of her hand on my face. She comes after me. Slapping me over and
over. My face on fire. I taste blood. Mine. I smile. She grabs my hair,
pulls me close, spits. Saliva runs down my cheek mixing with tears,
lands on my thigh. She pulls back to strike again. I plead silently for
mercy. Eye contact. She knows.

Gentle now, she wipes rage from my face. It's time. Her cock
finds my mouth. Slowly, rocking. Teasing, a bit deeper. Her head
tilted back, hands on the back of my skull, she strokes her cock with

my mouth. Pressure on the back of my neck, her cock reaches my throat, fills me, no room for breath. Pushing into me hard now, my eyes tear and spill. Pulse in my mouth steady, swollen. Sucking hard, wanting relief. She knows, pulls out slowly.

I fall to her boots, licking and sucking, breathing easily. Her boot comes up under my chin, my head strikes the coffee table. The bottom-fish darts from underneath, fins cutting my flesh. I scurry, hide between the coral and the futon. She chases me, her tail manoeuvring her through tight crevices until she is on me. She kicks at me, I curl tightly, become hard as a sea urchin. Angered, she pulls me out into the open, stretches me out. Soft spots exposed, she lashes into me with her harpoon teeth. My skin splits, blood is carried off as quickly as it pours from me. She has come for this. My blood. Her teeth stained red, she stands back, looks me over. I lie motionless.

She draws a circle with her finger and I turn around to give her my ass. Her weight bears down on me. I feel her hardness pushing my resistance away. Without warning she punctures me, filling my hole with agonizing pain. Try to relax. I wanted this, asked for it. She slams her cock in and out, I gasp for breath. Pain slowly turns to pleasure, I push against her, taking everything in. Tighten, relax. One hand on my hip, the other hand smearing my blood over her balls. Reaching around, fingers enter my mouth. I savour thick blood, swallow. She is like a merciless storm in my ass, throwing me side to side. I hear a throaty rumble and know she is going to come. My hands wrap around leather ankles and pull. Her shaft buried to her balls, she is thrusting as though her whole torso could slip inside. Both hands on my hips, bent at the waist. We crash to the sea floor, she shoots cum, body shaking. We lie still, panting, wetter than the sea engulfing us. Slowly she becomes soft inside me. We drift toward shore.

185

ZOË

The closer it got to show time, the harder it hit home.
My grandparents were coming to see this show. How could I
have been so cool with this for all the months between when
my grandmother said, "oh you're performing in the Bay
area, that's great! we can't wait to see you," and this
very moment.

The audience is milling in the theatre, placing
jackets on seat backs, going to the washroom, going for a
smoke, coming back, house lights up, music playing, clock
ticking. I rest sweaty palms coolly, one at each side.
Remember your words. Remember that you love this.
Remember that you're on in five minutes.

Oh shit, what if they hate this? I know I've put these
people through a lot, dashing any protective hopes they
may have had for a "normal" life for me. The least I could
do is spare them the raw honesty of what we do on stage.
It's not too late: we could be nice little queers. Maybe
Ivan could just cut that piece about being branded by a
shape-shifter with dragon's teeth. That piece where

Lyndell and I throw each other around the room in a sort of beast-like courtship, wearing boots and boxers and nothing else, will definitely have to go.

Christ, it's no use. we'd have to cut the whole damn show. Besides, I love that piece. That's it. I've really set myself up this time. It'll be more than any of us can take. They'll probably die this very night. "Grandparents rushed to hospital after San Francisco show, DOA due to information overload. Granddaughter called in for questioning."

Two minutes to show time. we slip in through the back door of the theatre and find our places. one minute to show time, house lights dim, music volume down and out, lights fade to black. Find your spike mark, I fish my stage glow from my gut, my words from my throat, lights up and .... oh yeah. This is what I love. The silence of people listening, getting it, laughing, tucking images in their pockets to take home with them to relish later. I love all of this, including reciting other peoples' lines under my breath in the wings while trying to watch the crowd's reactions from behind a bright spotlight. I love it when it's my turn. I love to play this crowd like the world plays me, moment by moment, line by line. From hours of frustrated silence in front of a blank computer screen to now, this is what it's all for, this is what I do.

An hour and a half of sweat and adrenaline and my nerves are long gone. Final bow and I am still riding high. This was a good show, well rehearsed. we worked hard on it. I think we finally got the timing right. It isn't until question-and-answer period that my uneasiness returns. The house lights are up now so I can see the faces of my family sitting in the audience. Their faces tell me nothing. They are listening politely to the questions and our answers.

we are beginning to thank everyone for coming and wrapping it up when a hand goes up in the area where my family is seated. it's my grandfather. my brother and i used to call him yoda because of his small, wizened appearance and his flexible frame. he was a high jumper in high school. he was diagnosed with bone cancer about six months ago and now he walks with a cane but his movements are still sharp and his wit hasn't been dulled by even a decibel. when he performed for me as a child, his ebenezer scrooge was as terrifying as his tiny tim was delightful. now he pushes all his weight through one hand into his knotty wood cane and stands. first i hear the growly tone in his voice, then i hear the words: "what did we do to deserve this?"

i look up at him, the great grandpa-god in the fifth row. i hold my breath until i see his face and then i laugh with relief. even from here i can see the teasing sparkle in his eyes. i guess there's no one in my family who can fully resist the spotlight.

The Apple
IVAN

Concepts being relative and context being everything, I am a virgin. There are places inside of me that have not yet been touched.

These are yours.

I will bend, stretch, bleed for you. I will feed the hand that bites me. I will let you have me, slip cool hands 'round my belly from behind, I will let you take me.

This is trust, proud-footed and sure.

All this I tell you with my eyes, bowed head, bent knees.

Your thumb tests my edges. A silver blade shines, flicks sharp behind your lashes. My hands move without me, they reach for you, attempt to touch the heat beneath your jeans. A steel hand in soft leather strikes my face, stops my breath, splits my lip. My tongue tastes blood. It must be mine.

A wound opens where your lips were, and you laugh, head back, nostrils flared. You are behind your eyes. Your voice is low, almost a growl. *How touching.* A gloved fingertip grazes my cheek, now bearing the hot badge of your hand. *How sweet.* A sneer dances on your upper lip. *Does it hurt right here?*

Your hand twists twice, *You don't really,* pulls up at the leather binding my wrists, *think I care,* your boot in my back, your hand a vice at the back of my neck, *what you want?* My face greets the floor.

I taste concrete, smell dust, the cement is cool on the side of my face.

And you are behind me. Pulling at the buckle at my waist. Fear creeps up my throat, claws at my tongue, bangs at the back of my teeth. My body has changed its mind/takes over/bucks/strains at leather chains. Someone is screaming, terror tears loose my tongue but I can't hear my words because someone is screaming.

And now I smell earth/dirt/leaves/decay/rain/blood/forest, and I am an animal/fur/teeth/caws/musk/panic/tongue rolling. It rages/howls/snarls, its teeth find flesh an instant before something stronger at its throat wants its life, now so precious.

It is the oldest game, the most ancient battle. The people of this forest do not want to hear this in the dark, they reach to reassure themselves, the young ones' sleep so innocent. This is mercy. Those who know swallow sharp stones, sit close, load sticks on the fire, pray their gods will soon bring daylight, it will stop. They are so naked, nervous, their teeth are dull, they move too slowly.

Fingers scratch thighs, jeans peeled back, my ass is an apple, red, white, bruises taste so different, don't they?

My own belt bites this fruit. It is all that has fallen, it is all I have left, and suddenly I want it, my last salvation.

But you will make me, take me, there there, that is not me, not that wet, that would mean I want your dick.

Inside me fire, inside me elbows scrape concrete forest. I am so young this is so old so many have been before me and now I know them they are watching me come.

Your hand in my hair pulls sweat my throat exposed your teeth are bare. You are smiling, I can feel it.

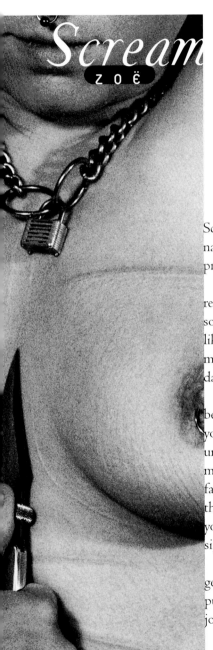

Scream
ZOË

Scream loud enough that I forget my name and remember that which can't be pronounced.

Give me a piece of your mystery to reverberate in my limbs when you're gone so that your sweet syllables might trickle like waterfalls, whispering memories to my muscles as they move through some daily routine.

Scream all the way to the door between sanity and self-knowledge until you can't negotiate the rules of a single unspoken game and launch winged demon moans from your soft, wet belly to fly you far away from all planned destinations to that soul island where you learn to love your fear and your so-called sin with every sigh and shudder.

Scream loud enough that I can't forget the way it vibrates, curve of bone and pulse of blood, until the next precious journey with a traveller wary of words.

Noise
Lyndell

I'm swarming in and out of
moodiness like the crowds of
people that swarm past. Caught
without consent in the whirling
brushes of snowblowers, market
racket and violent horns crashing
in on my once quiet shore.

Ironic really, that as I weave a
trail of my own fresh history
through the boisterous streets, I
could go the entire day and not
hear the sound of my own voice
spilling from my lips. My one
small voice released even in a
whisper might break the sound
barrier, push the noise level
beyond bearable and my ear
drums would shatter. I am moving without destination. The city
offers no escape.

I no longer turn inward for
rest. Noise has penetrated
through my flesh like a leech

and now resides in my internals. The sound of churning burns at my shallow patience. I know that silence has a distinct sound just as water has an unmistakable taste, sun a precise touch and fear an indisputable smell, but I've not the slightest sliver of memory connecting me to silence. Noise has consumed me, history and all.

I find stillness in you. Your open smile invites me to rest in your mouth. I accept. Our mouths meet and the connection separates me from my loud discomfort like green severs spring from winter. Your lips on me are like oil and the noise is water, repelled into the distance. I am stilled by you. You quiet my uncertainty, your touch answers questions I've never asked. You are soft and your smooth round corners so divine in this city of hard, sharp right angles.

Your breath against my neck warms me as strangers on crowded subway cars chill. In our silent embrace, your hand follows gravity and the shape of my back to rest on my ass, your fingers tighten, sinking in my flesh and making me taller with attentiveness. My hands slide with ease on your responsive oily body. My skin wanders through your fingers as you pull at my flesh, as though you were trying to stretch it open and submerge yourself in the warmth of my blood that only ten minutes before was as cold as the winter air.

Only you and I exist now. That, and the obscure feeling of razor-sharp safety. Our heated breath has dissolved invading sounds and I am conscious only of desire. I know that the city exists somewhere, beyond the corners of my mind, but I am too drunk in you to care.

Sometimes I wander back into life at just the right time and am reminded that fate wears no watch. I believe in fate and shedding blood for you and so I do not resist as my skin is tested by your hands. Your desire is loud, encouraged by my weight shifting into you. My eyes hide nothing. I am no longer numb with anonymity. I am fixated with the promise of noise-filled pleasure.

More powerful than the taxi's bellowing horn and the obscenities hurled out his window is the faint sound of your breath against my face. More colourful than billboards are your eyes, aglow with laughter. I can feel you inside me, wanting me as only new love can want. Your eyes tell all and of this I am glad.

With the approach of the streetcar, noise enters my consciousness again. I watch as you get on the car and disappear into the heart of the city and its chaos. I am standing alone on the street looking in your direction. People swarm around me, sleeves brush past, briefcases and bags bump my body. Above the sound of horns and cars, I hear the sounds of three million people around me. Sounds of people manoeuvring their way through the city streets with destinations heavy on their minds. I stand on the corner, at peace with the chaos, at peace with the stillness resting inside, at peace with my natureless surroundings. I realize that I'm whistling, contributing to the noise level and my ear drums remain intact. My heart is swollen, my steps light, my dimples exposed as I join the masses heading west, carving fresh history into the well-worn cement.

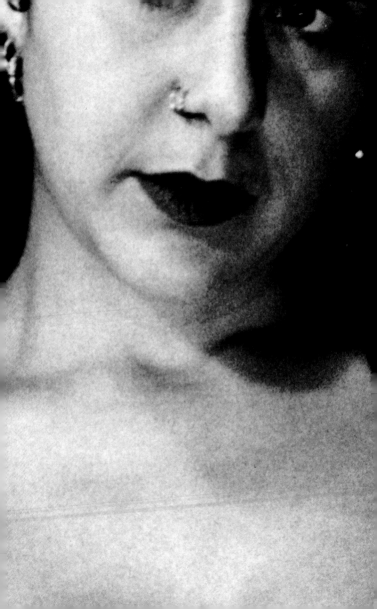

Things Happen in Threes

Anna

I.

this is what my mother said after her last car accident
this is what my grandmother said after giving birth to her third child
two years later, came the fourth

after my last failed relationship
this is it, i said, *things happen in threes*
knock on wood
think bright light
garlic and amulets, crystals, crosses, rosaries

i don't care if there are four seasons
i don't care if there's a joker in the deck
things happen in threes
i'm ready for tomorrow

just in case,
as an added measure
i have cleared my life of you
no photographs, letters, gifts
just memory

2.

when we loved each other
you appeared handsome   always
even though you seldom smiled

we fucked on church grounds in the country
green sun-lit fields stretched to the highway
mixed sweat with earth and complete abandon
the bell's echo wrapped us
stumbled out of the forest in shadow
unaware of the leaves in my hair,
the dirt on your knees,
until the faces of dismayed strangers offered up
a reflection and a prayer for us

we got lost in the woods more than once   you and i
became the children we had never been
you crouched in swampy lake edge
grabbed a garter snake
they are fast and slippery, but you, faster
"touch it," you chided,
as though it were a lightning rod

having inherited my father's stubbornness
and my mother's pride,
i swallowed my fear,
touched its shiny scales
dripping with sticky opaque fluid
glistening diamonds,
the smell more vile than skunk

scrubbed my hands with lakewater and lemon
you smirked and said
"the smell will fade, nothing lasts forever."

you were right.
nothing lasts forever
not scent, not love, not blind-sightedness
not even fear
and this is a good thing.

3.

My mother's regrets have never consoled me
nor have they replaced my own need to bleed.
I love the hand that bites me.

Hindsight is not twenty/twenty.
We lick our wounds with lies.
Had I known that you could not love me,
I would have loved you
more fiercely
more tirelessly
more.

199

Love is a near-sighted child
straining to touch stars
in an empty sky.
Time does not heal all wounds.
It makes them absurd,
softer around the edges
like a sepia-tint photograph.
Everything looks more beautiful, in the afterglow.

The Lonely Corduroy Boy

ivan

He says he doesn't remember when it started, that it was a thing that came to him before remembering anything began for him, or at least that's what it felt like, like he had always been like this.

He liked how it was soft one way when you rubbed it, and not so soft the other, but still soft. You know, corduroy is almost always soft, and he liked that about it.

He liked that the word itself was almost impossible to spell correctly, and that it looked right spelled wrong ten ways. "The word corduroy is kinda heavy on the vowel sounds, too, if you think about it," he says. That's another thing he liked about it.

He liked when it was new, when its pile was so … impressionable, showing slowly fading pressed-down places where he had leaned up against, or sat down on, or rubbed up against something for a while, marking himself softly with the moves of his day. And he says that he has just always been this way.

He thinks that corduroy should be worn as long as possible, worn until shiny spots appear on the ass of pants, even longer for shirts or jackets.

"When you run your finger sideways it has a totally different texture than up or down," he says. "Then it has contour, too, it has high spots and low places, wide ones, or not. No two are alike," he claims.

He liked that when he had been out in the rain and then crossed his legs for a while, silvery crisscross lines would appear, like ham wrappings, or like a velvet ass sitting in a string hammock in the afternoon sun for too long would look. These were just things that he liked, just always had.

He says he doesn't know which came first: the hard-on or the slow way the velvety lines stretched to reveal the spaces in between when the blood rushed under the skin there beneath the corduroy. A wide-wale covered woody was one of his favourite things.

"Junior high was a fucking nightmare," he said once, with serious eyes. "It was like 1976 or something, and I had to carry a duotang note-book around with me non-stop for about a year and a half," he said.

He can laugh about it now, but then again, pants are worn a lot baggier these days than they were in the seventies.

But it was always a private thing for him, not a secret, just a solitary thing. It wasn't until his late twenties that the thought of his skin plus corduroy, plus someone else's corduroy-covered skin up against him, ever crossed his mind. *Come to think of it, I always did kinda like it, whenever someone touched me, like stroked my arm, or rubbed my back or something, but I guess I never thought of it in terms of, you know . . . sexually before.*

"There must be other people like you out there," she told him over her mochaccino one day. She liked vanilla sprinkles and choco-late flakes, even almond or raspberry syrup, sometimes, while he drank black tea black. But they liked each other.

She had a bit of a thing for velvet and faux furs, and they had known each other since high school, from the island. They were in band class together; she played the trombone and he played the flute. She had wooed him by emptying her spit valve on the riser right behind him and then blinking at him in an innocently mischievous fashion, wearing a tight-ribbed sweater. They had had a brief but fun affair consisting of road trip school bus handjobs and backseat pants-on bump-and-grinds whenever he could borrow his brother's Tercel. They graduated before they went all the way. He went to col-lege; she didn't.

That was seventeen years ago. She travelled, did Europe, and South America, working summers as a waitress back home. She eventually went back to school, taking criminology while working three nights a week as an erotic dancer, a fact about her that amused him greatly. Now she was working as a parole officer, which he thought was hilarious.

They met up three years ago. He was working nights in her building.

"At least I'm not a sanitation engineer with a useless degree and my stepfather paying my student loans," she had said.

"I'm a janitor, you enforcer of our ineffective judicial system, and I've never regretted getting my degree in composition and arranging. I'm sure it will be of much comfort to me during my retirement. And he's not my stepfather, he's my mother's boyfriend. And I don't know how you can drink that this early. That's not a coffee, that's a fuck-ing dessert. That stuff will probably give you breast cancer," he told her, nodding at the cinnamon concoction floating on the foam of her coffee.

"Smoking makes your corduroys stink," she retorted, licking her long spoon and narrowing her eyes at him. "Go to a fetish party, for Christ's sake, and meet someone else like you. Do us both a favour, there must be someone else out there of the same persuasion—it can't be that hard. People can turn anything, however mundane, into a fetish, even corduroy." She removed her cup from its saucer and ges-tured toward him with it. "I'm sure you're not as unique as you think. You can't tell me that there's not a nasty young corduroy-covered vixen out there just biding her time, waiting for you to get over it, come find her, or stumble into someplace where she can find you and make her perverted little day. Go to a fetish ball. Trust me, I know these things."

"But it's not a fetish, really, it's more of a kinda … predilection," he said, fingering the thighs of his blue Denver Hayes.

"Whatever you want to call it, get thee to a Betty Page. You're boring me."

"You can be so cruel to me sometimes," he said, blinking with wounded lashes.

He   doesn't   like   the   word   trouser

"You just bring it out in me, you can be such a wet puppy some-times; I've never liked dogs. How's my lipstick? Jesus, what time is it? I've got to run, sweetheart. Say hi to your brother for me. Ask him if he's sure he's still gay."

After some consideration, he decides she was right. After some consideration, he slips on his light tan wide-wale pants with the low hips and the deep pockets, still hot from the dryer. He doesn't like the word trousers, is even less fond of slacks, but he can't help feel-ing kinda sexy in warm corduroy pants. He slides both his square-nailed thumbs beneath his wide leather belt, tips back on the heels of big brown boots and smiles like a cat in a mirror.

A plain white shirt then, because he is a simple man, really, not so much in mind but in taste. He feels exposed in loud colours, and confused by patterns or prints.

It was a Saturday night, and spring enough that he could smell the flowers on the trees. But it was late, and the air was winter nip-ple cold against the inside of his blue triple-wale jacket. He smoked and waited for bus #20, bound for downtown. He felt, for some reason, nervous. The bus smelled of warm wet bus, and he stood, standing-room-only style. The bus driver sounded tight-tongued in the intercom, urging everyone to push themselves into a space where there was no room for all of them to be.

He smelled her long before he saw her. From someone he caught a waft of vanilla oil, and something underneath that too, something fruity, in her hair, maybe. She smelled like cookie batter, she smelled of cranberry muffins, banana bread, something like that, delicious and definitely fresh baked.

He squeezed past a man who smelled of gin and mothballs—he had a good nose, for a smoker—to get closer to the smell of her. Was she the blond, with the bob and the faded Levi's? No. The redhead? *Yes.* The redhead. Copper curls that raced like snakes to her shoulder blades.

She smelled like angel food cake and looked like one of the devil's cherubs wearing overalls with wide brown straps. Corduroy

is   even   less   fond   of   slacks.

overalls with faded wide legs, ragged cuffs brushing boot heels, loose in all the right places, worn in the knees and stretched over her chest. Looked like she'd been wearing them for so long they'd become like skin on her, like without them she would be more than just naked, she'd be raw, red flesh revealed, her underneath unprotected.

He had always possessed an extremely keen sense of smell. He had always drunk black tea black and had always liked girls who played the trombone. He had always had a thing for corduroy, and he always did have a bent toward daydreaming.

Maybe she was a sculptor, or something. She had big-for-a-girl hands with a worn-right-in dirty look to them. If he could just get close enough to chat her up a little, they could talk about clay, or ceramics or plaster of Paris or chicken wire or Michelangelo, until, both enchanted with all their common interests, she would invite him to her studio on the run-down main floor of a house with a beautiful garden. They might end up in the common room in front of a bits-of-two-by-four fire, listening to Manu Dibango records, smoking homegrown and drinking her housemates' blackberry moonshine. And eventually they might end up lips on lips, hard parts in each other's hands, warm tan wide-wale and worn brown corduroy whistling together, his pager clacking against her pager, which buzzes silently between them at one point. They both laugh, trying not to wake anyone up ...

But what if the place of corduroy in her life stopped with merely wearing comfortable pants? What if she didn't know that corduroy was invented in the mid-1800s by the eccentric young and short-lived king of France, François Roy, le coeur de Roy? What if to her they were just another pair of pants? What if she asked him to take his pants off, explaining that the whistling sound made her teeth hurt?

Would she think he was weird? Would he feel humiliated? Would he feel dirty?

"Carrall Street," the bus driver barked, right after pounding the brakes and making the bus lurch to a stop.

He lost sight and then smell of her, as he pushed through to the back door and squeezed off the bus. He walked past where the old boot place used to be, past the pizza place, and hung a right in the alley.

It was the kind of alley farm kids dream of as the city, built when things were still made of red brick and wrought iron, sloped paving stones pushed up in places to give way to the occasional weed on the side, with graffiti and garbage garnish. Beautiful in a decaying kind of way, only the smell of piss hinting at the ugliness underneath.

He liked places you had to enter through the back door. In his dreams he was never the king, he was always the silent, immaculate butler, holding the keys to the back doors of everything, knowing all the secrets, from stable to throne.

He would have missed this back door entirely, though, had it not been opened from inside just as he passed by. A dark-eyed Viking-type with a handlebar mustache and an immense hand opened the door, then nodded a sombre goodnight to the pair who made their exit, a boy-faced androgen in a sailor's suit escorting a long-haired lovely who appeared to be wearing a skirt made entirely of black duct tape. Her skirt stopped just where her boots started, black stacked riding boots, laced long, up the front.

He stepped inside the door, blowing warm air into cold cupped hands. The Viking-type looked him over once, then glanced over to the doorlady, shrugged, and stepped back.

"Can I help you?" She raised a shaved and painted-back-in eyebrow at him, her red tongue resting dangerously between her too-white teeth, one long-fingered hand perched like a spider on the heavy wood table between them.

"Yeah, I guess I'd like a, I'd like to, you know … buy a ticket for the … party." He gestured behind her to the hallway, where a bored-looking boy scout stood waiting for the ladies' room.

"Do you know where you are?" she queried, and it seemed to him that her upper lip was now curled up ever so slightly, and the Viking behind him seemed suddenly closer, without having actually stepped forward. He moved closer to the table between them, leaned over it just a little, and for some reason he whispered.

205

"Yes. I'm at a fetish ball. A play party. A place to meet other …
I'm at a sex party."

"Exactly right," she smiled, but didn't seem any friendlier. "This
is a fetish ball. People come in fetish wear. You can't just get off work
from The Bay, or The Gap, or whatever, and come on down. We have
a strict dress-code policy in effect here, solely for the comfort of our
patrons, you understand. It helps to scare off the sightseer element,
you see? So you can go home and change into something more …
appropriate, or you can take off all your clothes and come on in."

He felt her eyes on him, heard involuntary blood rush past his
ears.

"Naked is also an option here, of course," she repeated.

"I'm a janitor," he said, as if this would explain everything.

"Uhh … come again?"

Both of her painted eyebrows were raised now, she was just about
annoyed with him, and the Viking had definitely moved, because one
of his ham hands was now resting on the boy's right shoulder.

"I don't work at The Gap. I'm a janitor. I'm here because I like
to wear …"

He looked directly into her eyes for the first time. She had stood
up from her chair, revealing a pair of shimmering chain mail pants,
and no underwear. He faltered but continued. "Thanks anyways. I'll
go home and … change, I guess. Maybe I'll see you another time."

And the door was shut behind him, its edges blending in so well
with the grime and spray paint that it was invisible again, just a low
base throb hinting at anything going on behind it.

It was raining harder now, and he turned up a frayed and soggy
triple-wale collar against the wind, lit a smoke, and stuffed one hand
into his pants pocket. He would walk home, he thought. He could
use the air and the time to think. But as the blocks between where he
lived and where he was stretched under his boots, and the wind
picked up, he found himself wishing that he were just a little more
… normal, a tad more mainstream. He even wished for a second that
he could just have been born with a regular old PVC fetish, or a bit

of a thing for rubber, or even trustworthy old leather. At least then he'd be waterproof.

But then he thought about the damp, silvery crisscross lines he could look forward to when he got home, and the ancient, comforting smell of wet corduroy, and he realized a beautiful thing that made him feel better. When you're wearing corduroy pants, you can whistle all by yourself.

a
b i t
o f
a
t h i n g
f o r
r u b b e r

Rush

anna

My body is a map.
I am the cartographer.
Desire, my language.
Sometimes I get lost.

Hours pass. I sit at my desk in faded
paisley flannels and a frizzed-out do
piled loosely on my head. Smoke a cigarette, sip on cold black tea, smoke
another. Watch the neighbours stack
eight cases of empty 24s into an old
pick-up with more rust than my uncle's
Chevy. That's a lot of rust.

I stare at my computer as though
she is an oracle. I wait for her to speak;
she hums. I punch out words: *Roses are*
pink, violets stink, I need a drink, 'cause I'm on
the brink ... I am desperately looking for
a place to start. Sometimes, that's all a
writer needs. My editor wants me to
write about desire. Desire, sure, I have a
lot to say about that, except all of a

210

sudden my muse has dumped me and moved to Saskatoon with a pin-striped self-help writer.

Highlights from my porn memory-bank flash like trees falling in and out of view in a rearview mirror. I'm looking for a phrase or image to jump-start my sluggish imagination: *beat my meat, juicy cunt, shoot your wad, hard nipples, wet lips, burning bush* ... This isn't helping. I need a new strategy; something more hands-on.

Before a performance, I get into character. Dress up and speak into a full-length mirror. It's not vanity—honestly. It helps create immediacy. Tricks of the trade also include indulging in moodiness and eating too much cheesecake. *So get sexed, Anna.* In the bedroom, I choose my favourite gear: black garter belt, leather G-string, my best stockings with runs, push-up bra, satin gloves, long boots and my full-length, velvet opera coat. Spin around in front of the mirror and scrutinize myself. Sexy, but incomplete. I apply mascara and a deep-red lipstick and arrange my curls. *All dressed up and nowhere to go,* I mutter, criticizing myself more thoroughly than anyone else would.

I sit in front of the computer again and wait for immediacy to take hold. I key in words: *My cunt is like a ... river. What does that tired metaphor mean? Flaming desire burns my ... panties ... bridges ...* God, I hate this! Damn editor! Why do I need to write about sex? I feel foolish sitting in my office like this, overdressed and late for the party.

Well, I didn't get all decked out for nothing. Determined to give myself something to write about, I throw my legs up onto my sturdy desk, slip my G-string aside and touch my smooth cunt. Freshly shaven and dry as a desert in August. Fine. Grab my bottle of lube and fill my palm. Slide my fingers up and down, close my eyes and trip through hallways, tongues, bathrooms, hands, bedrooms, bodies ... I can't hold on to anything. My fingers move lazily and stop. *I can't write about sex! Fuck!* I'll just tell my editor that I gave it my best shot and the result was nothing but a sore wrist, and a blank screen. I have plenty of other writing to contribute to the book. I already know she'll nod her head in an empathetic manner. That really annoys me.

I walk away, rejected by my fucking computer. So much for the magic that swims in a sea of words. I can't even make myself come! This is when writing feels like washing dishes. Clichés are useful here. *Tomorrow is a new day. Tomorrow is the first day of the rest of my life. Cheers to a brighter tomorrow.* Sleep really is the highlight of some days

I can't be bothered with peeling off garter, stockings and bra. I wash my lipstick off and fall into bed, where my lover is. She delivers light kisses on my shoulder blades. Her lips are a soothing balm.

"How are you, sweetie?"'

"Tired. Shitty. I couldn't string together three words to save my life. I need to sleep."

"Are you sure?"

"Have a look on the desktop. I'm sure, there's nothing."

"I mean, are you sure you need to sleep?" Her eyes shift to my breasts.

"Can't imagine doing anything else. Why are you looking at me like that?"

"Well … I was wondering if I could seduce you."

"I'd love to be seduced but I honestly think you have a better chance of winning the lottery tonight. You've got a fish out of water lying next to you."

"Can I snuggle you?"

"Yeah, I'd like that. Maybe you'll rub my neck?" I lie down.

"Sure. Close your eyes, lover. Relax."

She presses her body close. Rubs my knotted back. Grabs my hair at the root and pulls, gently at first, then harder. I love having my hair pulled. She knows this turns me on. My skin jumps. Half-lidded eyes flicker like headlights in the distance on a curved high-way. I don't want her to stop. She kisses me. Down my neck, over my bra to my lower back and into the soft valley of skin between hips and rib cage. She kisses my hand.

"Mmm. I smell your cunt. What were you up to in the office?"

"I was trying to write a sexy—" She interrupts me before I can whine about my writing again.

"Shhh. I wasn't *really* asking. I'll give you something to write about."

A part of me wants to bolt upright. I was tired. I said so. I was having a hard day while she was out having fun. *But I'm not tired anymore. I'm interested.* She takes my index finger and sucks. One two three fingers in her mouth, down to the knuckles. Four, in and out. *Am I wet now? I'm wet.*

"Do you know where I was this afternoon?" She's grinning.

"What? No."

"I took the dog to the park. On my way back, I looked up at the office window, and there you were. Legs up on the desk, spread wide open. I considered walking in on you, but decided not to."

"You what?"

"So, I let in the dog and went back out and watched you. You didn't get off, did you?"

"I can't believe you watched me. What if our neighbours saw? For Christ's sake!"

"Hey there, I was raised a good Christian boy. Leave Jesus out of this," she drawls coyly.

"You asshole. Next thing you know that greasy guy across the street is going to stalk me. I can't believe you did—"

"Do you want to get off?"

"You're a perverted fuck."

"That's why you love me. Do you want to get off? Yes or no?"

I feel betrayed. *She's such an asshole!* If she saw me, dozens of others probably saw me as well. *Did any of my neighbours jerk off? I can't say yes to her. I don't need to come right now, but it would feel good.*

"Well, which is it? Yes or no?" She glances at her watch like a banker on a tight schedule.

"Yes."

"Did you say yes?"

"Yes."

"Yes, what?"

"Yes, I want to get off. Fuck me."

She grabs my hair and pulls me onto my back. Whispers into my ear, "Bitch."

Before I can protest, she fills my mouth with her tongue. Deep, the way I like to be kissed. She snaps my G-string. I struggle between anger and desire. I want to push her off me and yell out *No! I am not your bitch or anyone else's!* Everything moves quickly. Both her callused hands have latex gloves on. She straps on a harness and cock. I love her cock. She slides her fingers easily into my cunt. Sucks and bites hard on my nipples. Waves of pain shoot up my spine. I buck. My anger is gone. I imagine people pausing, midstep, to look up at the window. I imagine wetness between strangers' legs.

"Aren't you glad I watched you? Tell me how glad you are. Tell me you want to be fucked more than anything else in the world. Tell me."

Goddamn her. She wants me to kiss her smug ass. Damn her. I want to come. That's all that matters.

"Yes, yes I'm glad. Just fuck me before I burst. Fuck me."

"Roll over onto your belly. Good," she coos. "Now say 'please.'"

"What? I haven't completely lost my mind. I will not say—"

She grabs hold of my hair and pulls hard. My back is arched and my ass raised high. Before I can berate her, she covers my mouth with her hand. Her cock finds my ass. My body tremors. This is what I want. She knows. Opens me up slowly at first, teasing my sphincter to the point of sharpness, until it eases and gives way. I push against her. We rush into a wide open space together. I'm covered in sweat. Obscene sounds squeak out my body. She holds on to my shoulders and eases into me with all her salt. I push back, offering myself. Her hands slide off my beaded skin. She grabs hold of my hair. *Damn hair. I'll shave it off tomorrow.* We swing like this until I'm screaming, "Fuck me, please, please fuck me."

"Oh God, oh God," she yells.

I come rushing forward, forcing her cock out, "Yes, yes, yes."

We collapse into the sheets. Our room smells like sex. She peels off the gloves, then the condom, and tenderly brushes hair off my face. We breathe hoarsely, smile foolishly at each other, unable to move.

"You took the Lord God's name in vain."

"I what?"

"When you were coming, you said, 'Oh God, oh God.' "

"Yeah, well, even a good Christian boy loses his head every so often. Besides, it was all in the name of helping you become all you can be. You have some new material to write about, and you said 'please.' "

"I did. I meant it. My editor would be proud."

My body is a map.
I am the cartographer.
Desire, my language.
I find myself.

Photo Credits

TALA BRANDEIS

Photographs, including details, on pages 16, 18, 19, 34–35, 36, 46–47, 58–59, 62–63, 76, 78–79, 86–87, 88, 92, 110, 126, 140–41, 143, 148, 149, 150, 155, 158–59, 169, 188, 218.

CHLOE BRUSHWOOD ROSE

217

Photographs, including details, on pages 2, 15, 32, 56, 66–67, 71, 75, 82, 83, 91, 115, 130, 136, 142, 144–45, 162–63, 166, 170, 173, 174–75, 181, 182, 186–87, 191, 192–93, 196, 200, 208–9, 212–13.

TRICIA MCDONALD

Photographs, including details, on pages 20, 23, 24, 26–27, 39, 40–41, 43, 48, 51, 53, 54–55, 95, 100, 107, 108, 116, 117, 120, 160, 165.

218

Acknowledge-ments

This book would never have been published without the hard work and encouragement we received from all the people who made the early live shows by Taste This possible. Thanks especially to Elaine Miller and *Diversity* magazine, Jeff Wonnenburg, River Light, Gillian Farnsworth, Kim Sirrs, Anne Williams, Dragon Xcalibur, Billy Lane, DJ, Lynne Kamm, Jake Dudas, Tyler Berrie, Archer Pechawis, Cynthia Brooke, Chantal Sundquist, the gang at 1626, Sherree Cleland, Krista Stott, Joseph Camilleri, Nahanni Diakun, Elaine Parke, Bet Cecill, Marianna Neumann, Eileen Ryan, Jennifer Lewis, D. Maracle, Stephanie Clarke, Jim and Marge Alcock, and Zoë's wonderful grandparents.

Big thanks also to a number of businesses and artist-run centres which helped us build great shows on a shoestring/horseshoe, among them Edison Electric Gallery of Moving Images, the grunt gallery, Harry's (off Commercial), the Lotus Cabaret, the Talking Stick Café and Gallery, Beyond the Edge Café, Video In Studios and the Western Front. Thanks also to Kiss & Tell for helpful tips, info and enthusiasm.

For their individual and collective contributions to this book we would like to thank: Tala Brandeis, Chloe Brushwood Rose, Tricia McDonald and Lisa Poitras for their stunning photography; Barbara Kuhne, Della McCreary, Irit Shimrat and Susan Stewart for their insightful feedback on the manuscript; Kate Bornstein for writing the Foreword and for being forward; Val Speidel for the great book design, and Persimmon Blackbridge for being everything we imagined in an editor, and more— patient, insightful and one hell of a wordsmith—thank you, Persimmon. Our heartfelt thanks to Press Gang Publishers for unwavering enthusiasm and vision.

220

TASTE THIS was born in the fall of 1995. They are a group of four writers and performers who, alone or in various combinations, tell stories, play the violin, drum and tin whistle, sometimes sing and sort of dance. They produce and direct all their own material, making it up as they go along. *Boys Like Her* is their first book, based on material written originally for performance then transformed into narrative fiction.

ANNA CAMILLERI is a queer femme writer and performance- and video-artist. Her fiction has been published in *Fireweed* and *Tessera*, and she recently completed her first play, *Red Luna*. In 1996 Anna won Honourable Mention in both the Montreal World Film and Video Festival and the Victoria Independent Film and Video Festival for *No Such Thing (as bad girls)*, which she directed, scripted and produced. She has worked as a television promotion producer, sex educator, alcohol and drug worker, set decorator and a whole lot in between. Anna dreams in colour.

IVAN ELIZABETH COYOTE is a writer, storyteller, tin whistler, lighting technician and performer. She has had stories published in Kate Bornstein's *My Gender Workbook* and in various small press magazines. She is currently working on her first video project and enjoys power tools and gospel music. Ivan hopes to run away one day and start a circus.

ZOË EAKLE got her acting training at York University, Toronto, and her training as a writer from documenting life. She has also worked as a set designer, set builder, craftsperson and painter. She was born and raised on a small island off Canada's wild West Coast, and is currently living in Vancouver.

LYNDELL MONTGOMERY is a composer of words and music and a multi-instrumental musician who has been practicing and developing her art for eighteen years. Lyndell composed the soundtrack for the film *No Such Thing (as bad girls)*. She is a member of Ember Swift, a self-produced and self-promoted band which concentrates entirely on original composition. They have toured Eastern Canada and played the music festival circuit in Western Canada. Lyndell is currently working with Ember Swift on a CD to be released in 1998.

PRESS GANG PUBLISHERS has been producing vital and provocative books by women since 1975. Look for Press Gang titles at good bookstores everywhere.

Selected titles

STORM CLOUDS OVER PARTY SHOES: ETIQUETTE PROBLEMS FOR THE ILL-BRED WOMAN *by* Sheila Norgate   ISBN 0-88974-080-1
Norgate's brilliant graphic rendition of etiquette rules from the 1930s to the '60s will have you laughing and cursing at the same time.

PROZAC HIGHWAY *by* Persimmon Blackbridge   ISBN 0-88974-078-X
An hilarious cyberlit journey through internet romance, pharmaceutical remedies for life and aging rebelliously. 1998 Lambda Literary Award finalist.

SUNNYBROOK: A TRUE STORY WITH LIES *by* Persimmon Blackbridge
ISBN 0-88974-068-2 cloth; ISBN 0-88974-060-7 paper
A humorous and lavishly illustrated novel about disability, mental health and passing. Winner of the Ferro-Grumley Award for best lesbian fiction in 1997.

HER TONGUE ON MY THEORY: IMAGES, ESSAYS AND FANTASIES *by* Kiss & Tell   ISBN 0-88974-058-5
This 1995 Lambda Literary Award winner is a daring collage of explicit lesbian sexual imagery, erotic writing, personal histories and provocative analysis.

LOVE RUINS EVERYTHING *by* Karen X. Tulchinsky
ISBN 0-88974-082-8 paper
Love and heartbreak, a Jewish family wedding and a CIA conspiracy keep the pages turning in this lesbian romance with a twist.

BEYOND THE PALE *by* Elana Dykewomon   ISBN 0-88974-074-7 paper
A landmark novel in historical fiction, this 1998 Lambda Literary Award winner is an extraordinary testament to the lives of Jewish lesbians who emigrated from Russia to North America at the turn of the 20th century.